To Mary Kate Whit... father on the Hawaiia... is everything she ha... drinks to excess, cons... of all, he mocks her faith. And yet she finds the captain of the *Moonflower* dangerously attractive . . .

Fired by his challenging taunts, Mary Kate determines to show him that the woman he calls a 'strait-laced little Puritan' has spirit! She is in danger of only one thing—losing her heart to a man who will never love her.

THE
MOONFLOWER
VALENTINA LUELLEN

MILLS & BOON LIMITED
London · Sydney · Toronto

*First published in Great Britain 1984
by Mills & Boon Limited, 15–16 Brook's Mews,
London W1A 1DR*

ISBN 0 263 74667 4

Set in 10 on 11½ Linotron Times
04–0584–65,140

*Photoset by Rowland Phototypesetting Ltd
Bury St Edmunds, Suffolk
Made and printed in Great Britain by
Cox & Wyman Ltd, Reading*

CHAPTER
ONE

FROM where she sat on the grassy hillside, her knees drawn up beneath her chin, the sound of the sea in her ears and the caress of a warm breeze on her face, Mary Kate had an unrestricted view of Honolulu harbour. It was a breathtaking sight for a girl born and raised in a town like Boston and she was grateful for her father's daily excursions here, however brief.

He came here to meditate and be close to the God who ruled his life. He was praying now, kneeling a few yards away from her, his face uplifted towards the clear blue sky, his eyes closed. His hands grasped a well-worn Bible against his chest and he had not looked once in her direction for the past hour. Nor would he until he decided it was time to return to the village.

Mary Kate's interest lay not in spiritual guidance, but in the ship she had noticed when they first arrived. It had been passing Diamond Head then, the most southerly tip of the island. Now it was nosing its way carefully through the dangerous coral reefs which protected the harbour from the seaward side, towards the bright golden beach and the hundreds of straw huts that was the village proper.

Very little stirred down there for it was still quite early. Apart from the fishermen who always went out before the heat became intolerable, few people roused themselves until late in the morning. What was there for them to do except eat and sleep, or sometimes entertain the crew of a ship in harbour? Life on Oahu in 1819 was far from strenuous, yet her father still insisted on rising at six a.m. and retiring at nine p.m., exactly as if he were in Boston. In between he made repeated, unsuccessful overtures to the islanders in his attempts to persuade them against their indolent way of living, the abhorrent custom of polygamy which was widely practised and their natural exuberance for the simple things which gave them pleasure—like eating, gluttonously most times, sleeping, with no thought for tomorrow, and making love. To be told that these three things which they most enjoyed were wicked and sinful was beyond their comprehension and he was mostly ignored.

Apart from local trading vessels from the other islands and a brig, just returned from Canton, which had departed the day after discharging its cargo, this was the only ship to arrive since they had set foot ashore. It gave promise of news from the outside world, goods to purchase, perhaps even material for a new dress.

Mary Kate and her father had been on the island one short month, but already their funds had been badly depleted because they had brought so little with them on the voyage and found it necessary to purchase a great deal more than they intended once they arrived, and attempted to set up a new home.

A few pieces of furniture, fewer clothes than she wanted to bring and a crate of books and learning materials was all he had allowed. He placed little store in worldly goods and had not allowed her to include anything he considered a luxury. They had the clothes on their backs, the knowledge with which to pass on the Word of God, money to buy food. God would provide whatever else He considered necessary, he had told her when she begged to be allowed to take a few of her mother's possessions. She had been dead less than a year and Mary Kate had loved her dearly. She had secreted away a book of pressed flowers, a gold locket and her mother's wedding ring—the only two items of jewellery she had possessed—into her own meagre case of clothing and said nothing.

Their arrival on the island of Oahu had not been greeted with enthusiasm. No one had made them welcome when they stepped ashore. No one wanted them, it seemed. They had been allowed to stay in the end on the sufferance of Kano, a not very important underling of the island governor. Both he and the King, Kamehameha, and the whole of his enormous court and anyone of importance, had gone to a royal wedding on the Big Island, Hawaii. There was no telling when they would return and Kano had no intention of arousing the anger of his royal master by communicating with him over such a trivial matter. They could await their return, or leave. It was of no importance to him. They had not been invited in the first place.

Five months spent at sea and eight thousand miles meant nothing to Kano who had never been further than Hawaii in all his forty years. Besides, they were not the first to come with their books and new ways, their talk of 'one god' when every *kanaka* knew there were powerful gods all about them—in the trees, the mountain streams, in fire and in the air they breathed. These newcomers never seemed to laugh and enjoy life and they always brought with them rules and regulations which greatly restricted the way of life of a people who were by nature pleasure-loving and amiable.

The zealous Pastor Nathaniel Whitney had inspected

the primitive native dwelling made of straw and thatch from the pandanus trees, windowless and crawling with vermin, which he had been temporarily allotted and thanked God for his good fortune. Thinking of the cleaning and cooking which was about to befall her as a dutiful daughter, Mary Kate was appalled and fearful as to their future.

She was hot and uncomfortable beneath the grey calico dress she wore buttoned high to the neck, but she dared not loosen it within sight of her father. Her red hair, as always, was pulled into a tight knot at the back of her head. It made her thin face with its high cheekbones and large eyes look even thinner, but she had been informed it was more respectable than having it flowing past her shoulders as most of the island women wore theirs. For an instant as she touched it she had the maddest impulse to snatch out the combs and let the fiery tresses tumble and blow free in the wind, to unfasten the hateful buttons, leave her father and run off into the forest amid the koa trees and the giant ferns to seek the freedom she longed for and had never known— never would so long as her father's strict moral code controlled her life.

She would never be able to break away from him now, and so she shut her mind against such distracting thoughts and shielded her eyes against the glare of the fierce sunlight dancing over the water. The ship had dropped anchor. With the King absent, there were not many other ships about. Without the royal barges and the flotilla of assorted boats, from sail-borne outriggers to his newest frigate, the new arrival had come in quite close to the shore. The deck teemed with men hauling in sail, opening cargo holds in readiness for unloading and making ready the longboats. What exciting places had it visited, she wondered, and why was its return so important?

She had been hearing gossip about it for the past two days. From the moment fishermen brought the news that the *Moonflower* was heading towards Oahu, its holds crammed full with cargo, there had been no other topic of conversation. Its arrival aroused a fervour of excitement among the villagers.

The Dutch captain whose vessel had preceded this one had been well received, had attended a *luau* in his honour, taking with him two hogsheads of rum on which most of the men and, to Mary Kate's horror, women too, had become very drunk. Her father's attempts to intervene at this 'drunken orgy', as the singing and dancing progressed throughout the night and huge fires roasted suckling pigs and cooked endless cauldrons of *poi*, so enraged the white sailors they drove him back to his hut with sticks and such dire threats of violence that he bolted the door behind him, voicing the fear they were about to be murdered.

But no one had found the arrival of the Dutchman's ship worth discussing and he had not been mentioned after his departure.

Most likely the captain of the *Moonflower* was a craggy-faced, middle-aged sea dog who made an enormous profit selling his hogsheads to the local grog-shop, allowed his crew to make free with the more than accommodating women until the ship sailed again and paid Kamehameha exorbitant taxes for being allowed to do so, Mary Kate decided.

Her curiosity had got the better of her that morning when she went to buy a cooking pot from the chandler's store, run by a dour Scotsman called Duncan MacIntyre. His kindness and that of several of the other local white inhabitants had made life bearable, if only just, those first frightening weeks. They had provided provisions, a few cooking utensils, two hard, but very welcome mattresses on which to sleep and pillows and blankets.

'Aye, the *Moonflower* is coming home, Miss Whitney.' His weatherbeaten face broke into a smile at her question. He had jumped ship after an argument with the first mate, hid in the mountains until it sailed, then settled in Honolulu. That had been ten years ago. Now he owned his own shop, had a 'brown' wife and three bonny sons. He was well content with life. 'There will be plenty aboard to interest you. Tapestries, tea services, materials from China, the finest you have ever seen. Ross Pendennis has a rare eye for beauty. You should see his woman . . . No, perhaps not.' He broke off as colour rose in Mary Kate's cheeks.

What an innocent! He could not remember more than two white women who had stayed long on the island. One had been the wife of a sea captain who had sold his ship and cargo to Kamehameha for a handsome price and settled inland. She had died in childbirth a year later, together with the infant. The other had been a Chinese girl abandoned by one of the ships. She had stayed three months and then sailed on a merchant ship *en route* for California. This one would not last that long, he decided, as the girl paid for her purchase and went out. If the fever did not get her, she would sell her soul to the devil to get off the island, back to civilisation, new clothes, a roof over her head that did not leak and people who spoke the same language.

On the other hand, the island might well reach out and touch her soul as it was capable of doing with the most unlikely people. She would never leave then, nor would she ever be the same again. She would be quite pretty, he thought, with more colour in her cheeks and a little more weight in the places that counted. She had lovely eyes—the largest most expressive blue eyes he had ever seen. He had never met her before her arrival on Oahu, yet the face had a vague familiarity about it. He searched his mind unsuccessfully for a long while and a customer dozing in one corner of the store, still trying to shake off the effects of the night before, which at the time had been most enjoyable but now only gave him a splitting headache, was suddenly rudely awakened as Duncan slapped a hand against his knee with a gleeful chuckle. Now he knew! The name was the same too. What a surprise that Bible-thumping preacher was in for!

'I did not bring you up here to daydream, girl.'

Mary Kate scrambled to her feet, smoothing down her rumpled skirts as her father's voice boomed out behind her. Lost in thought, she had not even realised he had moved. She flushed at the reproachful stare directed her way. She thought he had the coldest eyes she had ever seen. Flint grey, like dark storm clouds. There was never any warmth in them these days, only dislike for the daughter he tolerated because she was useful to him and for no other reason. Before Simon had left home he had been different. He had other aspirations then, with high hopes of his promising son. Now he had no one but Mary Kate. No son, no wife, only a daughter submissive and obedient to his will, fearful of his anger, the searing reproaches which could fall from his lips at the slightest human fault, the minutest failure to uphold his impossible standards. There was no love lost between them and they both knew it.

'There is a ship in the harbour, Father. I think it is the one the villagers have been talking about,' she ventured to say as she fell in step beside him and they began to descend the slopes towards the village. A vividly-coloured bird swooped low overhead, its raucous cry momentarily breaking the quietness which prevailed before it dived into the thick pandanus trees below them and perched on a branch, its head tilted saucily to one side as it watched them approach.

'You seem to have taken it upon yourself to find out about this vessel,' Nathaniel Whitney said, and his tone registered displeasure. 'Have you been gossiping with those women again when you should have been about your duties?'

'Those women' was the term he used when referring to the 'brown' wives of the traders and seamen. Women the men had taken as wives when they settled on the island, or the ship docked. Unions not recognised by God, or her father. Mary Kate had found the wife of Duncan MacIntyre friendly and helpful. Her husband had taught her English and it was a joy to communicate with her, but because she knew her father would never approve, she had not told him of the hours they spent together.

The devil rose in her again. The urge to torment him over the squalidness of their surroundings, their inability to teach these people about God or anything else. They were happy, which was more than she was. Why should they change?

'Are they not the very people we have come here to help?' she asked. 'If we are not willing to become part of their lives, how can we expect them to be part of ours? To accept our beliefs? If you can speak with the men and have them listen to you and I can do the same with the women, no matter who they are, then perhaps you will have your wish fulfilled and see them bring their children to us to be taught the Word of God. Surely you must admit it is a beginning, however unpleasant we consider it.'

'Unsavoury would be my choice of word, but you are right, I suppose. The women will lead us to the children and those are the ones important to us. Those poor, ignorant little beings who are crying out for our love. God's love.'

From what she had seen of the plump, carefree children who daily played in the village or on the beach, swimming, fishing, their laughter reaching her as she toiled in the hut trying to make it more presentable, or sat outside preparing food, for there were no facilities for cooking inside and she had to do so over a fire in the open as did all her neighbours, she would have said they were deprived of nothing.

'That ship,' her father declared suddenly. 'I have never seen the like of it before.'

Mary Kate's gaze followed his to fix on the new arrival. She knew little about ships, only what she had learnt from the waterfront while searching for Simon, trying to determine, without success, where he might have gone.

It was like nothing she had ever seen before either. It was a topsail, three-masted schooner, fore and aft rigged, with a square sail on the foremast. An adventurous craft for these unpredictable waters. It would take a good captain at the helm to control her, she suspected.

'We will not wait until the cargo has been discharged and the crew are ashore,' her father continued in a tone she knew well. 'We will go out to her, acquaint them with our presence. Perhaps we can stop their philanderings before they begin.'

After the last incident she despaired of intervening in the everyday life of the islanders. Kamehameha, during the later years of his life, had not objected to a very lucrative business with the ships which came to the Sandwich Islands, as they were known. Taxes were paid, cargoes distributed, and then there was that other, an additional tax which dealt with the accommodation of the local women. They were rowed out to the visiting ships early in the morning and returned to land at nightfall. Ships' captains chose their companions from among the daughters of local traders, paid a high price for the company of more highly-educated young women and often took them along when they left. The ones left behind were returned to their families without one iota of conscience being shown for the abandonment.

It was the way of the islands. A way Nathaniel Whitney chose to change. Even in four short weeks Mary Kate had seen enough to wonder if this was possible. This was how they lived. Had any outsider, however well meaning and dedicated, the right to try and change it?

There was a still darker side to the islands that she had only heard about. The traditional blood sacrifices to the gods which took place deep in the forests, in dark, grey-stone temples spoken of only in hushed whispers. Duncan's wife had told her little, but enough for Mary Kate to realise how perilous their position could become if they attempted to proceed too quickly—and blindly. Patience and hard work might overcome many of the obstacles in their path, but would it overcome the power of Kamehameha's high priests, put an end to the barbaric practice of killing enemy captives, do away with the many strict taboos on women which forbade them to eat such things as bananas, pork, coconuts and certain kinds of fish, and meted out death to anyone foolish enough to disobey them?

'Do you think that wise, Father? We do not know what kind of man he is, only that he appears to be quite popular among the natives. Would it not be better to bring him to the house? I could cook a meal if you wish. He might be pleased to have a little civilised conversation and if he has been here a long while, as I think likely, then perhaps we could ask him to intervene with Kano, have us given better accommodation, allow us to mix freely with these people. You know everything we do is watched and reported back to him. An unfavourable report to the King will mean our expulsion.'

She did not want to go on board, to be stared at by men who undressed her with their licentious gaze, whispered insulting suggestions as they brushed past her, deliberately touching her in a furtive manner. She had experienced it the first week she arrived and had run home in tears, but she had never mentioned it to her father. His answer lay in prayer, in the purity of her soul and mind. Her tears would only have irritated him.

'Popular?' Nathaniel retorted bleakly. 'I hear the man is a hard-drinking womaniser and he allows his crew to sink to the same level. He will not set foot over the threshold of my home. Of course these poor ignorant people welcome his ship. He'll bring them rum and gin, no doubt, with which to get drunk; pretty trinkets with which his men will seduce more unhappy young girls and then abandon them. Kamehameha will get his harbour dues and whatever else he can extort from them and everyone will think they are happy. I understand now why God guided my footsteps here. I have been given the task of bringing His word to a people in despair. I must show them what happiness really is. The joy of knowing the Almighty instead of placing their trust in a bottle. We will go down to the harbour.'

'Yes, Father,' Mary Kate said meekly and followed him as he strode down the grassy path like Daniel going into the lion's den. That was probably how he thought of himself, she realised. In his own way he was as misguided as the people he sought to convert, but she would never have dared tell him so.

It was an hour before they could get anywhere near the ship. It was already being unloaded when they arrived and they had to stand well out of the way as dozens of laughing *kanakas* staggered past them with crates and hogsheads, making their way rather unsteadily towards the village shops. By the reeling gait of most of them she suspected they had been paid in advance. The beach and waterfront was crowded with women and young girls, most of them dressed in their finest clothes. A few impatient ones, tired of waiting for the boats to fetch them, stripped off their *paus*, the colourful long skirts they wore, and began swimming out to the waiting men who lined the decks of the *Moonflower* waving them on and yelling words of encouragement.

She heard her father mutter something unintelligible under his breath and she turned away, her cheeks red with embarrassment at the sight of golden-skinned bodies running into the pounding surf. No one else thought it anything unusual, she realised, seeing they were the only two people to have given the incident more than a cursory moment of attention. Laughter and more shouting came from the decks as the first women were pulled on board. Suddenly the buttons high at Mary Kate's throat were painfully restricting until she felt as if she might choke.

The harbour master's outrigger came back to shore. She thought the little fat man looked very pleased with himself as he got out. More Spanish dollars for Kamehameha's pocket, with an additional bonus of several hogsheads of wine, a beautiful woven carpet and a bolt of exquisite flowered silk. The King's wives would fight for that item, she thought, watching it pass with a twinge of envy. Close by she heard her father remark,

'Your face betrays you, daughter. Do I not provide you with everything you need?'

She forced herself to look into those unfriendly eyes.

'It—it was so beautiful . . .'

'It will probably be used to buy a woman's favours. Remember that,' he rebuked.

'Perhaps it will be a gift, given in love,' she said and knew immediately her words had been ill-chosen as her father's face darkened angrily.

'You dare to use that word to me—here! With what is going on around us?' he thundered and his voice was loud enough to attract the attention of a group of sailors, engaged in conversation with some women. One of them made a remark which evoked hilarious laughter. 'There was envy in your eyes when you saw the cloth. What is in your heart when you look at these women?'

'Father, please,' Mary Kate gasped, embarrassed by the suggestion and horrified in case she had been careless and dropped her guard for a single moment, allowing him to glimpse what lay behind the façade of obedience. 'Don't shame me before all these people.'

It was his way. She had lost count of how many times he had upbraided her in public, often reducing her to tears when she was younger. Simon had been her champion on such occasions and with his guidance she had gradually learned to control her feelings, secrete them away into a private part of her mind which her father could not touch. Without him she had been so alone, so vulnerable, but in the end she had succeeded in her determination to be strong. To resist the iron will which not only repeatedly attempted to subjugate her, but to destroy the very essence of her being, reduce her to a shadow forever following in her father's footsteps without an identity of her own.

Seamen brushed past them with smiling girls on their arms, chattering noisily, laughing. They stood unnoticed as the *kanakas* continued with their job of unloading the *Moonflower*. A boat slid on to the sand which drew more attention than any of the others. Some of the natives dropped their bundles and ran to help the occupants alight as a crowd gathered. There was much bowing and rubbing of noses, which she had discovered was the customary greeting in the islands. A slim young man made his way across the sand, followed by a bevy of servants, all clearing the way ahead, wielding fly brushes which had the habit of landing across the faces of anyone who stepped in their path. Behind him came a woman whose long black hair fell almost to her waist. Her skin was softly tanned, the mouth full and sensuous, parted slightly as her companion said something which made her laugh, to reveal perfect white teeth. Unlike the majority of the island women who wore mainly only coloured *paus* with nothing above the waist except perhaps a necklace of coral, or shells or beads, sometimes with the addition of a cotton underslip for more formal occasions, this woman wore a scarlet *tapa*, material made from the paper-mulberry tree and dyed with berries. It was a breathtaking contrast against her hair and sunkissed skin, twisted tightly around her body in a most provocative fashion to cling snugly to lithe hips, emphasise a tiny waist and full breasts, covered, only just, by a pleating of the *tapa* before it fastened at one shoulder.

They were both people of importance, Mary Kate had decided as the group approached where they stood. There were several sailors with them. She saw her father's gaze settle on the tallest of them, who had an arm slung casually around the woman's shoulders. A stray lock of blond hair, bleached almost white by the sun, showed beneath a well-worn blue cap, set jauntily on the back of his head. His features were as dark as those of any islander. The face of a man who had lived many years on the island, she suspected, as Kano himself broke through the crowd of onlookers, and bent himself almost double, or as far as his huge stomach would allow, over the hand extended towards him. He repeated the process with the woman and then shook hands in a hearty manner with her companion.

'Kano, you've put on weight since I've been away.' The man gave a low throated chuckle and clapped him on the back. The gesture made Kano beam.

A far different reception from the one she and her father had received, Mary Kate thought. The tall man lifted his head and surveyed the faces around him. Finally they came to rest on the two figures standing well back, so conspicuous by their dress as strangers. He said something she did not understand to Kano and immediately the smile was gone from his face. Instinctively she knew that this was the ship's captain.

Nathaniel Whitney stepped forward, into the path of the oncomers.

'I wish to address myself to the Captain of that ship.'

'I am Captain Ross Pendennis, sir.' The blond haired man stepped to the front. He was six feet in height, broad-shouldered and not in the least perturbed by the frosty expression of the man he faced. The white shirt he wore, tucked into a wide leather belt with a large brass buckle, was open almost to the waist revealing a muscular chest as deeply tanned as the rest of him. The sleeves, rolled back past the elbows, showed a long, jagged scar on one arm. Mary Kate saw another, now he was closer, running across his right temple and disappearing beneath the cap. She could not determine the exact colour of his eyes, only that they were very, very dark. 'And who are you? By whose authority do you block the way of Prince Tamori?'

'By the authority of God.' A low murmur ran through the crowd at the arrogance of the answer and the Captain's mouth twisted into a smile that bordered on contempt.

'The only authority here comes from Kamehameha himself, my friend, so be careful with that careless tongue. If you are what I think you are, you will find no welcome here, from me, my crew, or the King. We have seen the likes of you before, although not many are foolhardy enough to bring their womenfolk with them.' As he spoke, those dark eyes came to rest again on Mary Kate. She felt as if they were gazing right through her, and quickly looked away. When she looked back, they were once again focused on her father and there was no friendliness in them.

Why had her father not been more tactful in his approach, taken her suggestion and invited this man to their hut where they could have talked in private? Now he had antagonised the very person whose co-operation he sought and probably offended a prince of royal blood as well.

'I need the protection of no man when I have that of God,' Nathaniel replied coldly. 'I have a duty to perform here and I shall do it, with or without your help. However, if we were to work together . . .'

'Dammit, man? What are you babbling about?' Ross Pendennis snapped. 'Take your Bible-thumping else-where. We don't need it here. Now stand aside and let us pass.'

'Let him go, Father,' Mary Kate said. 'The Captain is obviously a man who places little importance on human life. He ignores what does not affect his own particular way of life.'

Ross Pendennis stared at the slim, pale-faced girl who had spoken and his features were like granite. She had not moved him, she realised and prayed she had not made things worse. But his arrogance was insufferable!

'Heaven preserve us from do-gooders!' he said in a fierce tone.

'I do not like this man.' Prince Tamori spoke for the first time. His voice was uninterested. With a sweeping gesture of his hand he motioned to two waiting *kanakas* armed with spears, and they moved forward menacingly.

'Ross, wait! Don't let them be harmed!' A man came pushing his way to Nathaniel's side. Mary Kate stared at him disbelievingly. She had recognised the voice at once, but it was not possible! Not here of all places. 'I know them.'

'When did you leave the ranks of the ungodly?' the Captain asked, without humour. 'Well get on with it. Tamori isn't renowned for his patience when there's a hogshead of rum to be opened.'

The Prince nodded vigorously and smiled and it became clear to Mary Kate that his comprehension of English, even though he had addressed them in it rather falteringly, was not very extensive.

'Ross, Prince Tamori, Princess Lani, may I present to you my father, Nathaniel Whitney from Boston and my sister, Mary Kate. I don't know how they come to be here, I haven't seen them in three years. If I had never seen him again it wouldn't have mattered to me, but my sister . . .' The quiet voice, which held a hint of Irish brogue so reminding Mary Kate of their mother, flooded with sudden warmth as Simon Whitney crossed the space between them, caught her up in his arms and soundly kissed her.

'Simon! It can't be! It's impossible. Oh, it's wonderful, like a miracle.' She found herself laughing and crying at the same time, oblivious to anyone else as he hugged her close and she smothered his face with kisses. Three long years had separated them, but he had not changed. And yet he had, she saw, as she drew back from him at last and he wiped the last tears from her cheeks with his fingers.

The boy of twenty who had run away from home had become a man. The arms which had enfolded her were strong and capable. The sun-tanned face which regarded her was that of someone who had come to terms with himself and with the world. He was running away no longer.

'How—how are you here?' she stammered.

'I'm doctor aboard the *Moonflower*. It's what I always wanted to be, remember?'

How could she ever forget those dreams he had harboured since the age of twelve? The reason for many bitter quarrels with his father, and why he had stolen out of the house one night without a word and vanished from her life. She had seen him go. He never knew that. She had said nothing, rejoicing in the courage which had taken him out of the unhappy house to a new life. An adventurous life by all accounts.

'You—you are on board that ship?' Nathaniel asked.

No greeting for the son he had not seen in three years. No embrace, not even one flicker of warmth in those grey eyes. The son who had deserted him, and the vocation he imagined was his, had sought to instill in him despite all his protests and misgivings, the son he had travelled thousands of miles to find. But now he had found him he would not weaken and tell him, or show it even in the faintest relaxation of his stern countenance. 'You condone a way of life you know to be abhorrent to me? Do you share in their—activities?'

'As often and as fully as I can.' The answer came back at him with vindictive force. 'I'm married too. A Honolulu girl. I'd like you to meet her, Mary Kate. You'd like her.' He looked down at his sister and smiled, but she could not return the look. The fresh antagonism between the two men worried her, as it had always done. Only now Simon would not allow himself to be thrashed with a strap for disobedience, would not remain silent when his father began to talk of the future he had planned for him, as she knew he surely would once he had got over the surprise of his son's 'return'. She thought it a miracle they had found each other again. Nathaniel Whitney would consider it the answer to his prayers and would become even more impossible to communicate with on anything that was not of his choosing. 'I've a thousand questions to ask you. Is Mother with you? When did you arrive?'

'Mother died six months before we left Boston, which is why I am here.'

'I hope she died cursing him for the life he gave her, nothing but hardship and heartache,' Simon muttered, sending a baleful glare towards the silent figure a few yards away. 'I should have let Tamori's men split him in two, then you would have been free.'

'Don't talk that way, you frighten me,' Mary Kate declared. He looked for all the world as if he meant every word.

'He's a dangerous zealot who will do the same to you as he did to her if you let him,' her brother returned with a frown. 'We can't talk now, Tamori is getting impatient. He's been in a bad mood ever since we picked him up in Hawaii. He didn't want Lani to come on board, but with Ross there, fat chance he had of leaving her behind. I swear she would have swum after the ship if he'd said no.'

Mary Kate's gaze dwelt for a long moment on the beautiful Princess, now standing close to Ross Pendennis, a slender arm adorned with gold bangles thrown back to prevent the wind blowing her hair about her face. For a brief moment their eyes met and then the other woman looked away as if dismissing the newcomer as unimportant. Mary Kate suddenly felt very plain—and insignificant.

'Is she—his wife?'

'His woman. I don't believe Ross has ever given his heart totally to any woman, but she's been around him as long as I can remember and that's over two years.'

'She's very beautiful.'

'She's an insatiable she-cat, but I think, at times, she satisfies the wild streak in him.' Simon was suddenly serious. 'I'll have to talk to the Prince and try to make him believe Father isn't going to cause any trouble. You and I both know he is, and we'll have to cope with it if it gets out of hand. If the King hears any bad tales about him, you'll both be shipped off this island like lightning, and that's the nicest thing they will do to you. I've known a couple of incidents where the poor wretches were taken into the forest and never came back. Kamehameha has to be approached in the right way. I'll speak to Ross, he will know how to handle him. He'll go through Tamori first. Given the right approach, I could have you here for a long while. Would you like that?'

'You sound so hard. So unfeeling,' Mary Kate whispered. 'He is still our father.'

'For your sake, I'll remember that.'

'Do you have to ask this Captain of yours? I would rather we were indebted to no one.' Ross Pendennis, she suspected, was not a man to give favours lightly.

'He'll do it because I ask him, unless of course, you'd rather I found passage for you out of here as soon as possible.'

'A week ago I would have said yes, but not now. I don't want us to be separated ever again,' she whispered and kissed him on the cheek. Anything was bearable now he was by her side. 'If you told Captain Pendennis Father has come all this way looking for you and for no other reason, would he help us?'

'He'd laugh himself into stitches after seeing the reception I have just received,' Simon said cynically. 'But wait a minute. The idea would rest easier with the Prince. He's a sentimental soul especially when he's been on the rum, so we should have an opportunity to get to him tonight. There's going to be the usual *luau* for the ship's return. He'll be quite merry by dark. With any luck, we all shall.'

'Simon, that sounds awful.'

'It has to be done if you wish to make a better impression on him than you already have. Father insults him and you insult Ross, his closest friend. A bad beginning, little sister. Don't worry, everything will turn out for the best. And don't get me wrong. I love these islands and the people. I never want to be anywhere else.

When I'm at sea, all I think about is coming home. One day I hope you will find the happiness I have.'

'If you have both finished your welcoming speeches.' Ross Pendennis stood beside them. The derision in his eyes made her quickly avert her own. Had he heard her brother's suggestion and misconstrued its meaning? 'Simon, everything is ready for us at Duncan's and Tamori is parched. He won't wait a moment longer. By the way—' The dark eyes were intent on her face again, disturbing in their intensity. They were like two brilliant pieces of jet, she thought. Hard and somehow frightening. As if they were able to look down into her very soul and did not approve of what was there. '—Your father and sister are invited to the *luau* tonight. It's at Hakari Point. Tell them how to get there, will you?'

'I don't think either of them will be coming,' Simon said. 'My father will not approve of what goes on.'

'It isn't an invitation, it's an order. From Tamori himself. I convinced him your father is worthy of a second hearing, Lord knows why. That is what you wanted, wasn't it?' The last words were directed at Mary Kate. The announcement stunned her. Before she could stammer her thanks, he had turned on his heel and left them.

CHAPTER
TWO

THE *luau* was held in a sandy bay beneath the local beauty spot called Hakari Point. As soon as it grew dusk, people began to stream along the narrow, twisting mountain path which led to it, many carrying baskets of food. Liquor would be flowing in abundance, Mary Kate thought as her eyes fastened on the vast quantities grasped tightly under arms, even conveyed on hand carts. The local traders had done good business since the *Moonflower* arrived.

Her father had been adamant in his decision not to go. She had tried reasoning with him, to no avail. After dinner, which consisted as it did most evenings of a vegetable stew with a little of whatever meat they could afford, probably pork, he settled down in the hard-backed chair Duncan Macintyre had given him, the Bible open on his lap, leaving her to wash the plates and then join him. As was customary he would then read to her until it was time to go to bed, while she sat and sewed, her eyes aching in the light of the single oil lamp.

Someone laughed as they passed the hut and her thoughts were suddenly at the *luau*. The word meant feast and from what she had seen of the eating habits of the islanders, that was exactly what it would be. Part of her longed to be there, the rebellious part that was never content with the life she led. The continuous cooking and cleaning, the caring for a father who often was not even aware of her existence. The knowledge, if she was lucky, that she might someday marry and have a husband and children. Would she be loved then, or merely tolerated as she was now? Moved from one prison to another.

The other part of her tried to shut out such sinful thoughts. Men and women would be sitting together in the grass, eating, drinking, dancing. If their way of life was so morally wrong, why had God not wiped the islands from the face of the earth? These were His children too. Did He love them any the less for their wrongdoings? Was ignorance not a sin perhaps, but a virtue?

'Mary Kate! Father!' It was Simon's voice. Her heart leapt unsteadily. Had he come to fetch them? To confront their father if necessary? He was strong enough to do so now.

'Father.' Nathaniel had not looked up from the passage he was reading. He completed it, while she waited in an agony of suspense, before looking up. 'Simon is outside. May I let him in?'

'We have nothing to say to each other. Tell him I do not wish to speak to him,' came the cold reply.

'Well I wish to speak with you, Father.' The door was flung open and her brother advanced into the room. Behind him Mary Kate saw the tall figure of Ross Pendennis and hurriedly jumped to her feet, gathering up the sheet she had been attempting to mend. Pushing it behind the curtain which was all that separated her small bed and what little privacy was afforded her, from the main living-room and the bed where her father slept, she said,

'Come in, Simon. You too, Captain. I'm sorry, we were not expecting visitors.'

She watched the eyes of both men wander around the room and was swept with shame at what they saw. One table and two chairs, a moth-eaten couch which she had tried to brighten with several gaily patterned curtains brought from home. There was no comfort here, nothing to make anyone welcome when they stepped over the threshold. She knew she could have asked for more furniture from Duncan and his wife and they would have given it freely, but her father would not allow it. The bare essentials were all they needed. How her heart cried out for more! The room was as bare as her life. It contained no warmth—no love. She craved both with an intensity that sometimes frightened her.

'Good God,' Simon ejaculated, his disgust openly showing. 'You live here!'

'It was all Kano could find us,' Mary Kate spoke before her father, seeing the anger which rose in his face and anxious to avoid another quarrel. 'We—we have what we need. Things will improve when the King returns and learns we are here. He will understand our needs, I'm sure.'

'Unless you show yourselves at the *luau*, he will care nothing for your coming and even less for your going,' Ross Pendennis said sharply. 'Explain the facts of life to them, Simon, or do I have to do it.'

'Please, Ross, let me talk to them,' he pleaded.

'What is there to say that hasn't already been said, dammit! Tamori has ordered them to the *luau*. He is a prince of royal blood and a favourite of Kamehameha. He's been insulted once today and overlooked it because I told him they had meant no harm. He won't overlook their refusal to meet with him tonight.'

Six feet of manhood towered over Nathaniel Whitney's chair. Mary Kate thought he looked as if he might grab him and drag him up to Hakari Point if he refused again. 'As your host, Pastor, I have the grace to overlook your exceedingly bad manners, but Tamori is not like me. He is temperamental and given to bouts of extreme temper when someone like yourself is foolish enough to rouse him. God knows I have enough trouble with him then, over people I like. You, I don't know and I don't like! Get on your feet man. Where is the spirit of Christianity you have come to preach?'

Nathaniel rose to his full height, which was well below that of the man facing him. Such a challenge could not be ignored. Even though it would grieve him to walk in the midst of such sin, he would do so. Perhaps one person would respond to his words. One person saved was a beginning.

'Very well. I will come with you.' He put down the Bible, picked up his mahogany cane and, head held high, walked out through the door.

'In God's name, how did he ever sire you?' Ross asked, turning to look at Simon, who had been passed by without a glance. 'You are worlds apart.'

'You don't have to tell me that. Fetch a shawl, Mary Kate. We are going to enjoy ourselves this evening,' Simon said cheerfully.

'I'll wager you a hundred dollars, he won't allow it,' his companion chuckled and she stared daggers at him. He intended to spoil the evening from the start!

'I am sure you will be too otherwise employed to notice what I am doing, Captain,' she retorted icily and heard his laughter following her as she slipped past her brother into the cool night air. As mocking as the eyes which followed her.

The beach was illuminated by the light of many fires. The delicious smell of cooking reached them long before they descended to the sandy cove. There were about a hundred people present, she estimated. Half of them women from the village. The men were a mixture of *kanakas*, local men, traders and the usual hangers-on from ships that had sailed, and sailors from the *Moonflower*. All, it seemed, were approaching the evening in the appropriate mood.

Whole pigs were spitted and roasting over several of the fires. On the others, there were fresh fish, *poi*, and some kind of stew that was being tasted with relish by the men cooking it. Some people were swimming in the calm water, some lazed beside the fires, or in the cover of the rocks nearby, others were slipping away to more secluded places until the food was ready to eat. Time was unimportant. This was a night for relaxation, feasting, making love. The presence of two outsiders among them bothered no one because the Captain had brought them with the approval of Prince Tamori.

Mary Kate was amazed at the amount of food which was spread out on the straw mats and large ferns which served as tables. There seemed to be mountains of bananas, coconuts and pineapples. She wondered where the latter had come from as she had seen no sign of any growing near the village. There was breadfruit, yams and fresh fish. Lobsters and crabs.

She saw her father cast a disapproving eye in the direction of the hogsheads of rum and other spirits which were momentarily attracting the most attention and she tensed, expecting the usual critical remark.

'Will you have something to drink, Pastor? Nothing intoxicating, of course,' Ross Pendennis asked, as if anticipating something of the kind. 'A little *awa*. That's what we call the local brew here and it's quite harmless.'

'Nothing. Thank you.'

'Suit yourself.' He gave an indifferent shrug. 'What about your daughter?'

'She does not drink either, Captain. I came here to meet with the Prince. That is my sole interest, not joining you in your evening of debauchery,' Nathaniel said, in a tone that had often made his parishioners tremble in their shoes. It had no visible effect on the Captain.

'Would you care to raise our wager?' Ross drawled amusedly to Simon, who grinned and shook his head.

'So you gamble as well as drink to excess, Captain. I have been told you have a woman too.'

Mary Kate caught her breath at her father's audacity.

'It's no secret, Pastor. I'm human, although some of my crew might tell you different. Tamori and his sister are by those rocks ahead. Simon, bring us some drinks, will you? If we keep him happy he may look on the Pastor in a favourable light.'

'Come and help me,' Simon murmured, taking his sister by the arm and drawing her aside, leaving Ross and their father to continue alone. 'Don't worry about them. Ross is in too good a mood to allow tactless remarks like that to get through to him. How long have you been wearing your hair like that? You used to wear it loose, tied with a ribbon. Like Mother did when she was younger.'

'This past year.' Mary Kate raised a hand in a self-conscious gesture towards her hair. Why did he have to make that comparison? 'Don't you like it?'

'It makes you look like an old maid. Father's idea?'

'He prefers it this way.' She knew the reason and Simon guessed it too.

'I don't. He's not looking this way, have a drink.' He thrust a glass towards her. 'Go on, it won't kill you. It's *awa* and harmless, but I warn you, it's rather an acquired taste.'

She tentatively sipped the dark brown liquid and instantly her face contorted into a grimace.

'Ugh! It's bitter! Like vinegar.'

'Give it to me, I'll find you something else.' He swallowed it and then turned back to the long trestle table which was covered in dusty bottles and jugs. 'Let's see what we have here. Rum? Whisky? No, I don't think so. Too strong for you, little sister, I have to break you into this new life very gently. Duncan's fruit punch. Now, that's better. Here you are.'

'I shouldn't,' Mary Kate protested. 'If Father sees me he will be furious.'

'I'll tell him it was goat's milk,' Simon chuckled. 'Drink it down and then we'll take these four jugs across to the others. The food is beginning to smell good. Are you hungry?'

'After living on stew and fruit for most of the time we've been here? I'm starving.' The fruit punch slid down her throat like nectar. Nothing stronger than tea and milk had passed her lips before. Her father allowed no alcohol in the house. Even when her mother became ill and the doctor suggested a tot of brandy in warm milk at night for her, it had not been allowed. 'What is that funny looking sauce being put on the pig?'

'It's a paste made out of *kukui* nuts. It makes all the difference to the taste.'

'I must remember that. I'm looking for ways to make my cooking more appetising.'

'After tonight you may not have to do any.'

'What do you mean?' She looked at him curiously, but he only smiled.

'I'm saying nothing more, only that I'll move heaven

and earth to keep you near me. Come on, let's join the others.'

'Can't we talk for a while? There are so many questions I have to ask.'

'Ask them later when we've eaten something. Once the *kanakas* wade into the *poi* and my shipmates start on the pork and kid, we shall have to fight for our food.'

'*Kanakas* are natives of the islands, right?' She picked up a jug of wine and followed him.

'Full marks. What else have you learned in your four weeks? I spent a long while talking to Duncan at the chandlery this afternoon,' he explained as she opened her mouth to ask how he had known. 'He said you've had a pretty rough time. We both know whose fault that is, don't we?'

'We have managed. Don't be angry, Simon. You know how he is. He'll never change. Life with him will always be difficult wherever we go. I'm resigned to it now.'

'The hell you are,' he swore and she winced at his sharpness of tone. 'You are nineteen years old with the whole world at your feet. You could leave him and start a new life somewhere else. Marry perhaps.'

'And who would want plain Mary Kate Whitney, who isn't good at anything very much at all? I go from day to day being careful what I say, how I act so that we don't argue. You taught me that, remember. Say nothing.'

'I was wrong. I should have punched him in the face long ago and taken you with me when I left. You'd be settled now. In California or San Francisco. Maybe even England. I've been there, do you know that? Ross showed me the village where he was born, near a place called Polperro in Cornwall. He hadn't been back in sixteen years, that's when he and his father and mother sailed to come and live here. She died during the voyage. He said the place hadn't changed a bit, but he didn't want to go back. He's as much a part of this island now as Tamori and as unpredictable at times. He's the best friend I've ever had. Saved my life the first time we met. I was trying to get a job on a ship, any ship. I was stupid enough to offer money to a seaman on the waterfront. Four of them followed me back to my lodgings and would have killed me if Ross hadn't heard me yelling. Not many people would have launched into a fight the way he did. He was pretty badly cut with a knife. Did you see his arm and temple? I almost got him killed too. Now that's enough of being serious. I want to know what you've learned.'

'Hardly anything. Duncan's wife has been helping me. She's sweet. Most of the other women have stayed well away from me. Father frightens them, I think.'

'He'd frighten old Nick himself.'

'I know the name of the skirts the women wear—*pau*. The material and that of the *tapa* is made from the bark of the paper-mulberry tree. *Aloha* is a greeting. Now I know *awa* is that horrible drink. *Hale* is a house. What is *wahine*? I heard someone call me that this morning. Is it nice?'

'It means woman. They probably called you *haolewahine*. Foreign woman.'

'Yes, that's it. How am I doing?'

'Very well. You give me the impression you're very anxious to learn their language.' He gave her an admiring look.

'I must. We want to set up a school. I will have to be able to talk to my pupils won't I? What is it? You look sceptical. I was going to be a teacher once, remember?'

'Until Kamehameha gives you permission to stay, you

must do nothing. The old ways rule the lives of these people, Mary Kate. They live by strict rules and to break them often means death. Ross is well established here. He has a fine house and lands given him by Kamehameha and his father before him. He has introduced change into their lives in a small way, but over many years, and he never pushes to get what he wants.'

'Like Father does. You mean we must be patient.'

They weaved their way through the dancers and Mary Kate managed to evade the persistent sailor who had followed her, trying to grab her as his partner, before they reached a cluster of rocks where the Prince and his party reclined on large mats. Half a dozen of his stoutest warriors stood guarding them in a semi-circle, while servants offered food and drink. The Princess' personal maid was in attendance, constantly fanning her mistress with an enormous palm leaf. She looked stunning, Mary Kate thought, and she was aware of the fact. Her *tapa*, which again left bare her shoulders and arms, was of white silk. Except for a necklace of pearls she wore no jewellery. She needed none to enhance her natural beauty and there were many men present who were probably envying their captain, she thought.

Stretched out beside her, so close that her body touched his whenever she moved, he looked relaxed and very much at home. Once or twice the black eyes surveyed the festivities as if to assure himself all was progressing well and the moment that happened, the instant the woman watching him felt his attention slip away from her, Mary Kate saw her deliberately say something to bring it back to her. Or she would lay a hand on his arm, stroking the skin with long, slender fingers. Her nails were long, and painted with henna.

Like talons. Ready to scratch out the eyes of any rival. Somehow Mary Kate could not envisage her being ready to give up the pleasures of life for the Kingdom of Heaven. She was in a heaven of her own making and loving every moment of it. She looked away as he bent forward and kissed the full mouth offered to him. No rubbing of noses for the Princess Lani!

'Does she give you the feeling she'd like to eat him like a Black Widow spider does its mate?' Simon pulled his sister down beside him, whispering in her ear as he did so. 'Your cheeks have some colour in them. It must have been the punch. You'd better have some more.'

'I will not,' she protested as he reached for the jug. 'Simon, no! Father's watching.'

Her brother picked up one of the wooden cups being used for drinking, filled it with wine from one of the jugs and then deliberately raised it in the direction of his father with a broad smile. As he expected, Nathaniel's face grew cold and he turned away, resuming his conversation with Tamori. Immediately Simon pushed the cup into her hands.

'Quickly. Good girl.' He nodded in satisfaction as she swallowed several mouthfuls before handing it back. 'I'll make a normal human being of you yet.'

Ross Pendennis saw the swift exchange and a smile tugged at the corners of his mouth. Here was the Bible-thumper preaching to Tamori and his own daughter was indulging in the very sinful practice he was seeking to stop. His amusement deepened as he watched Mary Kate laugh at something Simon had said. Not for one moment did he believe she was as pure as those innocent blue eyes proclaimed. All women pretended innocence at first, but that soon vanished. He suspected she was longing to have another drop of Duncan's fruit punch, which to his knowledge was always liberally laced with whisky.

He knew little about the girl or her father, only what Simon had told him one night when they were drunk together, a short while after he joined the *Moonflower*. He hated one and loved the other. Ross had envied him that close commitment to one person. Although he considered the young man to be a close friend, he had never really been attached to anyone since his father died. They had sailed side by side for many adventurous years and he sadly missed those times. No woman could fill the void left by his death. He had tried that at first and decided they were all fickle and as treacherous as his mother had been. So he had settled for a ship instead. The *Moonflower* was his real mistress. Far more trustworthy, more satisfying than any woman could ever be. When he was at sea, she was all he desired. When he was in another port, he was as unfaithful to Lani as he knew she was to him.

Women came and went from his life without leaving any impression. Lani had been his mistress for two years, but he knew he could leave her tomorrow and care nothing. Love was not a word in his vocabulary. Love made a man weak and vulnerable. He did very well without it. But he did not envy or ridicule people like Simon who had a pretty wife and hoped for a family, or his crew who took their pleasures where they found them, as he often did. It was a way of life most of them found satisfying and uncomplicated. His rigidly enforced rule, however, that no woman be abandoned without provision being made for her, made him popular among parents who found themselves with a pregnant daughter on their hands. The work he constantly gave to the *kanakas*, breaking new ground and tilling fields which were planted with essential foodstuffs shared by all, ensured the well-being of everyone connected with him. Simon aided the sick in the village where dysentery, leprosy and drunken brawls were rife. They came to him with their grievances, hoping he might intervene on their behalf with Tamori and often he did.

'You find the *haolewahine* interesting?' Lani's lips caressed his cheek. She nibbled at his ear until he jerked his head away irritably. The way she was always so possessive in public annoyed him, even when he was in a good humour. He looked into the beautiful face and saw jealousy mirrored in her brown eyes. 'I do not think I like her.'

'She's none of your business,' he answered. 'She's Simon's sister and for his sake you will be polite to her, if nothing else.'

'You forget who I am.' Lani's eyes flashed warningly. Only Ross never quailed before her anger, the cruel streak in her which at times drove her to turn on those about her. Servants feared her. None remained with her for any length of time. Either she dismissed them or they met a more permanent fate. The young girl with her now would have to go, she decided as she looked up and saw her eyes were fixed on Ross Pendennis. She considered him a possession to be shared with no one. Hers alone until she discarded him.

Ross knew her better than she imagined. Tamori, her half-brother, had acquainted him with all the unsavoury facts he knew about her the moment he realised they had become lovers. It changed nothing for Ross. She was the most beautiful woman on the island and he appreciated beauty. The desire which always arose in him when he remembered how voluptuous and satisfying her body was and the pleasure it gave him whenever they were together was enough to maintain the relationship. He allowed her to think she owned him because it was of no importance to him. He knew otherwise.

'You will do as I say, my little she-cat, or I will turn you over my knee and soundly spank you,' he said quietly. She drew back and said no more, knowing full well he was serious. Close by Tamori lifted his head and stared at them, wondering how Ross put up with her displays of jealousy. Their conversation had been in the island dialect which he had understood.

He had hardly heard a word Nathaniel had said to him. He was bored and more than a little tipsy. He did not want to give up his rum or his gambling or his wives. Why should he have only one wife when he could have five? It was the law. To be changed by the King, not this man who he he did not like.

One of the sailors produced a fiddle and began to play, encouraging more people to dance. Mary Kate found herself smiling as she watched the sailors trying to teach their partners strange new steps. She had found the island dances slow and graceful, a pleasure to watch. Young girls were distributing wreaths of flowers, slipping them over heads as they passed. Simon grabbed one and placed it about her shoulders. She smiled at him gratefully. He was determined to make the evening enjoyable for her and he was succeeding. She felt a little lightheaded, but cast aside the thought that it might have been the punch. She had only had two glasses, after all. It was the excitement, she decided. This was all so new and fascinating to her. She had never dreamed everyone could be so friendly.

Duncan and his wife and sons were seated a few yards away. They had acknowledged her when she passed them, but they did not join her now. Her father did not

approve of the woman at the Scotsman's side and
Duncan would never have embarrassed her by risking a
snub. How she wished her father could bend just a little.
The fact that they were sitting with the Prince and
Princess might carry some weight in the future and make
their task easier. She longed to get to know more people,
to learn their tongue and their customs. To be a real part
of this new world she was living in. It had not been of her
choosing, but she intended to make the best of it.
Simon's arrival had erased many doubts and
apprehensions as to her ability to settle here from her
mind. With his help she would manage it.

'Damn the man,' Simon growled. An hour had passed
during which she had eaten her fill of roast kid and
seafood. She had refused another cup of punch. Simon
was drinking enough for them both, she saw, and did not
like the way his skin had become flushed and angry. He
was watching their father and growing more tense with
every moment. 'He's not talking to Tamori, he's dictat-
ing. Ross was right, it won't work. Either Tamori's too
drunk or not drunk enough. If Father doesn't stop
quoting him Bible passages, I swear he'll blow a blood
vessel.'

'Patience, Simon,' she pleaded.

'If only he would have some food or a drink. He's
insulting him by not doing so.'

At that moment Ross rose to his feet and came across
to where they sat, bringing another jug with him. Simon
held out his empty cup asking tersely,

'Do we stand a chance?'

'It's difficult to say. You know what Tamori is like.
Unfortunately he's taken a dislike to the Pastor from the
start.'

He upended the jug and swallowed several mouthfuls,

his gaze thoughtful as he stared past the flickering fire to where Nathaniel sat with the Prince. Shrugging his shoulders he took another drink.

'What exactly were you hoping for, Simon?' Mary Kate asked. She could smell the whisky on them both and it was beginning to make her feel uncomfortable. She had never seen her brother drunk and she did not want to.

'You didn't tell her?' Ross asked, showing mild surprise.

'I wanted it to be a surprise. If Tamori spoke to the King about you and Father, his opinion would carry great weight,' he explained to his sister. 'Ross told him how close we were and how he has come looking for me to make us a family again.' Simon almost choked on the words. Mary Kate wanted to tell him how true they were but knew this was not the time or place. 'We were hoping Tamori would invite you both to his village until Kamehameha returned. Ross has said you could stay at his house.'

'Don't hold out any great hopes that there will be an invitation,' Ross interrupted. 'That bored look on Tamori's face is indicating he feels it's time he got down to the serious drinking and eating.' He waved forward a *kanaka*, whispered in his ear and the man went away, returning minutes later with an enormous platter of assorted roast meats, small fish wrapped in *ti* leaves. Another man followed with the Prince's personal drinking mug brimming over with rum. It was a china mug, the handle in the shape of a hunting dog. Rabbits chased each other around the base in what was intended to be a hunting scene. Ross had brought it back from England for him. His face lost its bored expression and he beamed at the Englishman and promptly gulped back the contents.

'Does he always drink like that?' Mary Kate gasped. Even her father was too thunder-struck by what he had seen to make any comment, but as the mug was promptly refilled, he rose to his feet, gave the Prince a jerky bow and turned away.

'I am doing no good here. It's time we went home, daughter.' He looked down at Mary Kate, ignoring both Simon and Ross. She did not know if he was angry or dismayed he had achieved nothing. His face registered no emotion.

'The night is young, Pastor. Why don't you sit down with us and enjoy what we have to offer you?' Ross suggested in a cordial tone. 'I grant you the surroundings and the people are not what you are accustomed to, but you could grow to like it if you give yourself a chance.'

'Give Mary Kate a chance,' Simon said. 'Let her stay with us. We haven't seen each other for three years, nearly four. I don't think we shall be able to corrupt her pure spirit in a few short hours, do you?'

'Simon, don't! I don't know you when you talk this way. You are different.' His sister frowned at the outburst. It was the whisky talking.

'I'm a grown man now,' her brother returned. 'As you are a grown woman. He has no right to run your life for you. Think for yourself, dammit! Tell him you want to stay and have fun like the rest of us.'

'Please, Father. May I?' she pleaded, knowing what the answer would be.

Nathaniel stared down into her upturned face and his eyes grew accusing as they fastened on her flushed cheeks.

'You have been drinking. Get up, girl, before you disgrace us both. If this is how your brother conducts himself, then that is up to him. You will not see him again unless I am with you.'

'Father, no!' She could not believe her ears. 'You can't mean that.'

'He means it.' Simon scrambled to his feet. He was not very steady. His hands clenched into tight fists at his side and he looked as if he was about to hit his father. Mary Kate caught his arm.

'I'll go home, Simon. Don't let your evening be ruined.'

As she stood up a young sailor approached, swayed past Nathaniel and faced her. He held a long stick in one hand which he laid at her feet with a low, sweeping bow which almost unbalanced him. She was aware of a sudden hush falling around her. Her father was frowning, Simon looked as if he could not believe his eyes and the Prince had sat up, his interest aroused. To one side of her men and women were sitting in a circle, Mary Kate saw. A man would rise, carrying a similar stick to the one before her, and place it at the feet of a woman. It was some kind of game, she thought, and wished she knew how to respond. She was bending to retrieve the stick and hand it back when Ross said, his voice choked with laughter,

'For heaven's sake, girl, leave it where it is.'

'Why? It's a game, isn't it?' she asked in all innocence.

It was several minutes before he had composed himself sufficiently to answer and by that time Tamori, Lani and the whole gathering were convulsed with amusement, that began with loud giggling from the women and burst into roars of hilarious laughter as the men joined them.

'My apologies, Miss Whitney.' He did not sound in the least sorry she thought with mounting confusion, followed by anger. 'Young Stephen has had a little too much to drink. He meant no harm. He simply wanted you as his—companion for the night.'

'It's a game,' Simon insisted as she stood stunned, horrified. 'A harmless game. If the woman doesn't like the man she doesn't pick up the stick and it's given to someone else, but he had no right to try it on you. I ought to . . .'

'You will do nothing, Simon.' Ross's voice cut across him like a whiplash. 'Everyone is pretty merry, that's all. Go back to the others, Stephen. This one would probably read you passages from the Bible all night and that wouldn't keep you warm.'

The sailor grinned good-humouredly, returned to the circle and presented the stick to a teenage girl. It was promptly accepted and they both ran off into the darkness hand in hand.

'And this is where you wish to stay? Among such evil?' Nathaniel stared at his daughter, quivering with suppressed rage at the incident. She stood there without a word. 'Have you no shame?'

'You can hardly blame her for what happened,' Ross snapped. The evening was well on the way to being ruined with this man's presence. 'Go home, Miss Whitney, before your innocence is further disgusted by the sight of people enjoying themselves.'

'No, you will stay and see for yourself what kind of people we have come among,' the Pastor thundered. 'You must be taught a lesson. Come home when you have witnessed enough.'

Abruptly he spun around on his heel and walked away, ignoring the jeers and caustic comments from the crew of the *Moonflower* which followed him.

'I must go with him,' Mary Kate whispered to her

brother. She no longer wanted to stay. The evening was ruined.

'He's given you the chance to break away from him,' Simon protested. 'You don't have to go back to that pitiful little hut. When we sail tomorrow you can come with us, can't she, Ross?'

'If she wishes. It will cause trouble though. It's best they both come together or stay here. Let her go, Simon. Don't you realise how far apart you've grown over the years? Your world is different from hers now.'

'She's my sister. If she stays, then I do too.'

'And abandon Kiki? No, you won't, that's the whisky talking, boy, and you know it.'

'Don't call me boy.'

'Then don't act like one. You see, already we are quarrelling. She's trouble and I won't have that,' Ross said bleakly. 'Walk her home if you must, but be on board when we sail tomorrow or I'll come and fetch you—and you wouldn't like that.'

From behind them Tamori made a remark in between mouthfuls of pork. Most of it fell out of his mouth on to the embroidered robe he wore and was brushed away by a hovering servant. Ross looked startled. He went and crouched on his heels beside the Prince and Mary Kate saw him gesticulate as if in protest. Then he shrugged and rose to his feet.

'Tamori has changed his mind. You'll come with us tomorrow. Both of you.'

'What made him change his mind?' It took several minutes for the words to penetrate Simon's befuddled brain.

'Who knows.'

Ross Pendennis knew, Mary Kate thought as their eyes met, but he was not going to tell anyone what the reason was. It did not matter. Her father would have what he wanted, a chance to turn the islanders from their sinful way of life and she would be with Simon. For the moment she did not want to look further than that.

'Thank you, Captain.' Ross looked at her quizzingly. 'I know you don't want us causing trouble, as you put it. You could have argued with the Prince over this, but you didn't, and I am grateful.'

'You don't argue with a Prince of the royal blood, especially with the connections this one has with the King,' he replied. 'It is an order, Miss Whitney. You and your father are expected to obey it. I have no say in the matter. I wish I had. He's amused by new faces. He'll tire of you both before too long, I'm sure of that.' His sarcasm squashed her moment of pleasure and she took Simon's arm, thinking how much she disliked him.

'Take me home, please. We must tell Father.'

'That I shall leave to you. Be sure to tell him it's an order, not a request. It cannot be refused. That will ruffle his feathers, but he'll come just the same. He won't be able to resist the challenge. I don't care so long as we can be together. You'll love the house and Mamalou. And Kiki, that's my wife . . .'

'I was right, you do like her.' Lani came to Ross' side as he watched the pair of them walk away. He could hear Simon still gaily chattering long after they disappeared from sight and once again he found himself envying the bond between them. So different by nature, yet bound together by chains stronger than any blood tie. 'I heard what my brother said. You asked for them to come to our village as a favour to you, knowing he would not refuse you, his *aikane*—his friend!'

She spat the words at him, her lovely face contorting into an ugly mask.

'She's Simon's sister. That's reason enough. They will have a while together before Tamori tires of the Pastor's attempts to convert him and he kicks them off the island with Kamehameha's blessing.' Ross was unperturbed. Tamori had been highly amused when he made the suggestion. Lani was growing more and more possessive, he had said, what Ross needed was a woman he could rule as women should be ruled. This red-headed *haolewahine* was perfect for him. She had no spirit. She would make a wife and mother and never once complain if he looked at another woman, or went off on long sea voyages as Lani did. His wives would fatten her up so that she was more presentable and found favour in the eyes of his friend.

Heaven forbid, Ross thought. What had he done? What had motivated that stupid request? For Simon's sake or his own? Now why had that absurd idea entered his brain? Mary Kate Whitney, while it might prove amusing to strip her of that façade of purity, was not his kind of woman. And he had made it a rule never to complicate his life unnecessarily.

'Don't question my motives again, Lani. I don't like it,' he added sternly as she sidled closer to him and her full mouth deepened into a sulk.

'I thought you were growing tired of me.'

'You witch.'

Picking her up he deposited her back on the mats and stretched out beside her. Without being able to define why, he had broken his own rule and his life was about to become complicated with the arrival of two do-gooders, who would no doubt turn idyllic bliss into a mortal sin. But then Lani entwined her arms about his neck and began to kiss him and soon the touch of her body became far more of interest than Mary Kate and her father.

CHAPTER
THREE

THE *Moonflower* was not only a sleek, fast ship, but as
Mary Kate discovered when she went aboard next morning, there were comfortable cabins below decks to
accommodate five or six people, as well as the crew.

Ross's Chinese cook, a wizened-faced little man with
a long pigtail, who chattered incessantly as he served the
food, uncaring that no one present understood a word he
said, had laid breakfast in the panelled dining-room.
The dark oak wood gleamed, silverware shone in the
early morning sunlight streaming through an open window. The whole room smelt of fresh polish. It reminded
Mary Kate of the way her mother had spent hours
polishing their own furniture with loving care, shining
what few silver items they possessed.

Ross Pendennis had scarcely given them a glance as
Mary Kate followed her father below, but she had seen
his mouth deepen into a smile. He had been so sure they
would come. Tamori retired to his cabin, his head still
aching abominably after the previous night's orgy of
drinking and eating and his sister, after taking one look
at the three figures seated at the long table, immediately
returned on deck, her expression registering extreme
displeasure.

And so Mary Kate, her father and Simon ate alone
that morning. The first time they had done so together in
nearly four years.

Mary Kate still wondered at her father's change of heart. He had said nothing when she told him of the Prince's 'order', but he had looked decidedly stubborn and her hopes sank. Simon had all but lost his temper when his father refused to speak to him and left the house, vowing his intention of returning to the *luau* and getting very drunk with his friends. He had done just that, Mary Kate suspected, from the way he pushed aside his half-eaten meal and grimaced as she accepted Chin Ho's offer of more scrambled eggs and coffee.

Her father had risen before her. His books and papers had been put away into the box which had brought them and his clothes lay across the bed ready for packing. She had not asked how or why he had agreed, it was enough that he had done so and her heart sang as she made preparations for their journey.

She felt no sadness at leaving the hut which had housed them since their arrival, only at leaving new friends like Duncan and his wife behind. He had come to see them leave and had given her a parting gift of a pretty necklace made of shells his sons had gathered from the beach. He would see them soon, he told her, as he often visited Ross Pendennis and collected many items for his store. She assured him she would be looking forward to it.

Simon finished his coffee and then rose and went across to the sideboard which housed an assortment of decanted wines. Mary Kate was aware of her father's back stiffening visibly as he heard the chink of a glass.

'Will you not join me, Father?'

Nathaniel climbed to his feet and slid his chair back under the table with a jerky motion. His mouth was compressed together in a tight line. He never drank and well his son knew it, nor had he ever touched a woman other than his wife. He considered sins of the flesh in the same light as he did the taking of another human life. The ultimate sin that damned a man's soul to the eternal fires of hell.

'I am going to my cabin to read. Where will you be, daughter?'

'With me. I'm going to show her over the ship. It's only a short journey, but I might as well make it as interesting as possible,' Simon answered. The wine eased the dull ache in his head and took away the sour taste of whisky from his mouth. He had forgotten how much he had drunk, only that Ross had carried him back to the *Moonflower*. He had awoken on his bunk without knowing how he got there.

'Simon, must you antagonise him?' Mary Kate protested softly as the door closed behind her father. 'You haven't given him a chance since you met.'

'I need nothing from him now. I have my own life. I'm trying to see that you have one too, out from beneath his heel. Don't let us quarrel, I'm in no shape for anything energetic, believe me. Let's go on deck and I'll give you a guided tour.'

Mary Kate had never been on a ship before she stepped aboard the one which brought her to the islands. The long journey had often been tedious, uncomfortable, and she had suffered badly from sea-sickness. The *Moonflower* was so different. It barely seemed to touch the water. Its sails billowed in the wind, fascinating her. The sound of the sea, the wind, the call of a bird, were all about her. With a contented sigh she leaned on the rail beside her brother, her eyes shining.

'I think I understand now why you love this life.'

'It isn't always this peaceful,' Simon chuckled. He was pleased at her interest in everything he showed her. It brought them still closer together. He would force a wedge between her and his father if it was the last thing he did. It was the only way to save his sister from going the same way as their mother, becoming as she did in later life. He had enough saved to take her to California, send her to school so that she could become a teacher. She would meet some man and marry and settle down to a life of her choosing. He was determined on it. 'I've been in my fair share of rough weather. I still go green.'

'I don't believe it. You, the ship's doctor? How did that come about, by the way?'

'I signed on as a crew hand after Ross rescued me from those thugs on the waterfront. The *Moonflower* had a doctor then, a Frenchman. Damned good he was too, but there was an accident while we were sealing off the Californian coast. He was among several men injured. Somehow I found myself taking over. What I had to do with those men didn't come from what I'd read in books, but with the Frenchman's help and guidance, I got all but one of them back into shape. The accident left one of his hands useless. He taught me everything he knew and when he retired and went back to Paris, Ross asked me if I'd like to take his place.'

How proud he sounded, Mary Kate thought, and he had every right to feel that way. He had accomplished a boyhood dream. Was it not possible their father would feel the same pride as she did for his achievement? It had not been easy for him. It deserved praise from them both.

'I am so pleased for you.' She leant up and kissed him on one cheek. A passing sailor whistled saucily and Simon quickly drew away from her.

'I see the beady eyes of my captain on me, reminding me I have work to do. Half the crew are spending their leave in Honolulu where there's more activity. So we are short-handed. Do you want to go below with Father?'

'I'd love to stay here if I won't be in the way.'

Simon glanced along the deck to where the Princess Lani was reclining on a *tapa* mat, being fed sweetmeats from a silver dish. Occasionally she would raise her head and stare up at the tall figure at the helm, or wave a serving girl closer for a sip of wine from the cup she held.

'No more than she is. That one is trouble.'

'The Captain seems to like that kind of trouble,' Mary Kate replied. She too, allowed her gaze to rest on Ross Pendennis, not for the first time since she came on deck. She had not seen him once look her way, yet she was sure he had. She had felt those dark eyes following her. It was the most uncomfortable experience.

He stood with his legs astride, one hand on his hip, the other on the wheel. He seemed to be staring straight past her, but she could not be sure. He had been born out of his time, she thought, as he turned his head and looked up at the sails. That sun-bronzed face was almost piratical. His attitude towards women certainly was. Capture a prize, enjoy it and then discard it after its usefulness was over. She was not so naïve as to believe Lani was his first mistress or that he did not have other women when he went away on his travels. He was a privateer, living his life to the full, enjoying the spoils of war and the opportunities which arose for a quick profit. Simon had told her his house was like nothing on any of the other islands. He lived there like a king, his authority undisputed.

Did the Princess stay there too, she had ventured to ask, and wondered why afterwards, for she had no possible reason to be interested in the relationship she shared with the English captain. She learned that Lani lived in a large house with Tamori on the far side of the village they were heading for. It had been built originally as a copy of Ross's home, but before it was finished, Tamori had tired of it and changed the style. It was large enough to accommodate his wives and himself and Lani and her servants and more than fifty guests, but lacked the elegant grace of the original.

After Simon had left her, she wandered along the deck, not minding the stares and comments which at times followed her. They were rough, ignorant men, but they were his friends and so she ignored them. She found herself at the stairs which led up to the raised bridge and the wheel. Should she? Dare she? She mounted the stairs as if drawn by an invisible force and found herself not a yard away from Ross.

'You have eaten well, I hope? Chin Ho gave you everything you wanted?' He asked the questions without looking at her. He was watching Lani and the expression of anger on her face as she realised who was beside him. The next few minutes would be well spent, he thought wickedly, and turned to give Mary Kate his full attention.

Her cheeks were glowing, those large blue eyes alight with something he could only guess was excitement. Was it the journey which had roused her or had one of the crew been trying to make an assignation? He had warned them what he would do if any of them got involved with her and brought down the wrath of Nathaniel Whitney on his head. What he brought upon himself, was another matter.

He smiled and Mary Kate was suddenly aware how different it made him look. Younger, boyishly handsome, yet despite the disconcerting smile there was still something in the depths of those eyes which made the colour rise slowly in her face. A hardness. A challenge?

She wondered why he had asked about her comfort, when she knew full well the little Chinaman had been with him only a few minutes before and had no doubt been asked the same questions. Was he wishing to find fault with her or her father? Did he regret already the impulsive gesture that had made him accept the Prince's ruling without argument. Simon had been as surprised as she was at his change of mind. Or did he have an ulterior motive for giving way so easily? Perhaps he hoped her father would arouse Tamori's displeasure and be sent away. What other reason could there be?

'I like your ship, Captain, though I confess I know little about them.' If she was pleasant, perhaps he would be so too. She had nothing to lose and if she could win him over to her father's side, make it possible for the two of them to talk . . . 'I think you are in love with her. The way a man loves a woman.'

'Do you now?' The dark features creased into an amused grin. How wicked those eyes could look. 'What does a child like you know about love?'

'You do not have to insult me, Captain,' Mary Kate gasped.

'Why not? When we first met you accused me of being, and I quote, "a man who places little importance on human life. He ignores what does not affect his own particular way of life". Believe me, Miss Whitney, human life is very important to me, especially my own. If I have offended you it is no more than you deserved. Come now, admit it.'

'If—if I was rude, then I apologise.'

'Oh dear, you have no spirit after all. Lani would have threatened to have me whipped, or thrown to one of her hungry gods. All you do is say you are sorry. Dear God, where is your backbone? You are not like Simon, are you? He says what he thinks and the devil take the consequences, despite his upbringing.'

He escaped and learned to fly free with the birds. I have never had the chance. Mary Kate bit back the words, aware he was watching her with narrowed gaze. She hated him for that. He had been the same at the *luau*, watching her, wanting to send her home like a little girl while the grown-ups enjoyed themselves. He had made her feel so insignificant. More than that—insecure. She had never felt this way before, never considered a way of life other than the one her father had planned for her. Now Simon was back in her life and she had begun to be happy again and then this man looked at her and she knew doubt and uncertainty and yes, fear! So sure of himself, so strong-willed. He was incapable of any decent feelings where a woman was concerned and blatantly displayed his mistress on deck to proclaim it to everyone, yet she knew, without a doubt, he was the most attractive man she had ever met.

Attractive and dangerous. He was constantly challenging her, if not with words, then with the way he looked at her. Challenging her faith to remain strong and undaunted against the force of his personality and all he represented. Now she knew why he had not objected when Prince Tamori had invited them to be his guests. He wanted to destroy both her and her father. In some way disgrace them before the islanders and the one man who could speak well of them to Kamehameha. Once that was done, he would be rid of them.

She would fight him. Not his way, but her own. He would learn that Mary Kate Whitney had spirit!

'Simon has not been feeling too well this morning, Captain. He must have enjoyed himself when he re-

turned to the *luau*.' Bright blue eyes, wide with innocence smiled across at Ross. 'How is your head this
morning?'

'I'm sorry to disappoint you, Miss Whitney, but I
don't have a hangover. After you had gone I was far too
occupied in another direction to drink further,' came the
outrageous reply and she heard him chuckling loudly as
she gathered up her skirts and descended the stairs with
what little dignity he had left her.

Simon rejoined Mary Kate as the ship dropped anchor
off a quiet cove. She could see Diamond Head jutting
out into the sea way off in the distance and deep valleys
in the midst of bright green foliage. Towering behind
them, some so high their peaks were forever swathed in
white mist, were slate-grey mountains. It was midday
and growing uncomfortably hot. Simon wiped a hand
across his perspiring face as they watched the boats
being prepared for launching. He gave her the impression he was eager to go ashore. She was curious to meet
his wife and discover what kind of girl had captured his
heart so that he had no thought of ever returning home.

A crowd of people were gathering on the yellow sands
awaiting the arrival of the first boat.

Among the *kanakas* who had brought with them
mules to transport the cargo from the *Moonflower* to its
final destination, one man stood out as being of singular
importance. Flanked on both sides by a personal guard
of armed warriors, he stood with folded arms looking
towards the ship. A magnificent cloak of yellow
feathers, some tipped with scarlet, covered his shoulders
and trailed in the sand behind him. Mary Kate had
learned enough to know that only personages of royal
blood or of great importance were allowed to wear the

feathers of the Mamo bird, which was seldom found outside Mauna Loa on the Big Island.

'Men from Ross's plantation,' Simon explained, 'and Kalakui, by the look of it, probably here to greet Lani with a bunch of his cronies. He's a kind of high priest. He dabbles in a bit of everything. But for him I think Tamori would have been more receptive to new ideas. Kalukui and Lani keep him pretty much under their thumbs. She was Kalukui's mistress before she met Ross. Some people believe she still is. Lani is too ambitious to let go of anyone she feels will be of use to her. Most of the villagers are afraid of Kalakui. He has complete domination over most of them and his word is law. Tamori's too weak, or too scared to make a stand against him. Kalukui and Ross are deadly enemies. Ross laughs at any idea of Kalakui and Lani plotting to get him off the islands and take over his property, but I've seen those two with their heads together. They are dangerous and powerful. He should take more care.'

'I do not think your captain is afraid of anyone or anything,' Mary Kate said. Ross Pendennis had left the wheel and was moving in their direction. Deliberately she turned her back on him, as if she had not seen him. She had not forgiven him that little scene on deck some while earlier.

'Take our two guests ashore first, Simon. I'll send Tamori and Lani in the second boat and stay a while to supervise the unloading. I've some fine statuettes below and I don't want them broken before they get to the house. Go on ahead—no, send one of the *kanakas*. Tell Mamalou we shall have extra mouths to feed. You make sure everything is unloaded safely and packed on to the mules. Your sister will make a good sailor. She must come with us again some time,' was his parting shot before he walked on, leaving her inwardly fuming. Nothing could ever get her aboard his ship again. In fact the sooner they parted company the better. Then she suddenly realised he had offered them the hospitality of his home. She would have to put up with his odious company still longer.

She sensed, as in Simon, a change in her father's attitude as they reached the shore. He had not spoken to her or her brother since they left the ship, but his gaze had been speculatively considering the landscape and people ahead of him. Perhaps he would be different here, Mary Kate thought, a spark of hope rising inside her at the interest flickering in his eyes. This was not the challenge that had faced him in Honolulu, but it was a beginning. Simon had told her the village itself held no more than a hundred people, nearly half of them under the age of thirty. Which was why Kalakui had been having trouble over the past year. The older generation still believed fervently in the old religion and would do nothing to upset their very vengeful gods, but the younger ones had begun to question the blood-sacrifices, the strict taboos, the power of life and death which the King held over them and used ruthlessly.

Tamori, being young, could be swayed either way with the right handling, Mary Kate thought, and again her hopes lifted. If her father was tactful and approached him carefully, they might have their school after all, a place to open those minds not yet closed against new teachings—a new God, more powerful than Kamehameha, far more benevolent. As she stepped ashore she offered up a silent prayer that her father would have this chance. It was the first time she had prayed since leaving Boston. It was as if in those first few moments when her feet touched new ground, something was reawakened in her, bringing her close to the faith she had all but abandoned on that long voyage which took her from the land of her birth, everything she knew and loved, to a strange land, with a father who did not love her. That did not seem to matter any more. Uppermost in her mind was the thought of a school where she could be what she had always wanted to be—a teacher. God moved in mysterious ways. Had he a purpose in bringing her here too?

'What on earth is in all those chests?' she asked in amazement. At least twenty had been brought up on to the land over the past hour and there were still more waiting to be unloaded from the *Moonflower*. Pack-mules waited patiently for their burdens, while men humped and heaved their crates and boxes around them. Tamori and his sister had retired to the shade of some trees on a hillock, Mary Kate and her father had sat on the sand and watched Simon supervising the arrival of the precious items. Statuettes, Ross had said. She was curious to see them, but she knew she must show no sign of it before him. She had to stay as far from his world as was possible.

'A few little knick-knacks Ross has brought back for the house, and his friends.' He looked significantly towards the two figures beneath the trees as he spoke. 'This is our biggest load yet. We won't be going to sea for a while. We had some rough weather this trip, so he has told the crew they can have a couple of months' shore leave. The ship is going to be overhauled and refitted for our next trip to Canton with a cargo of sandalwood. Wait until you see the material I've bought for Kiki . . . and a real bone-china dinner service. Why do you look like that?' He smiled down into his sister's startled eyes. 'Did you think her an ignorant savage with a bone through her nose? That we ate off the dirt floor perhaps?'

She knew the angry words were meant not so much for her as for his father and so she did not reproach him.

'Is she pretty?'

'I think so, but then I love her. I can see Ross coming ashore. I can get these things on to the mules now and then we can leave. It will be dusk before we get to the house.'

'That long? I had no idea.'

He waved a hand towards a ridge of mountains behind them. In the brilliant sunshine there was nothing sinister about those gigantic volcanic peaks, but after dark, Mary Kate decided, she would not like to walk alone near them. They were the sleeping place of the old gods, the myths she and her father had come to destroy. Shrouded in mists and mystery and death. A place to be avoided by the wise.

'Our valley lies just in front of those. It's a beautiful place. The land is good, there are streams and a lake. We live well. It's like paradise. You'll think so too when you see it.'

'Paradise is not of this world, but the next,' Nathaniel said, rising to his feet and brushing the sand from his trousers.

'Yours perhaps,' Simon returned. 'I've found mine and I'm content with it.' He was unrepentant in his happiness and she knew her father could not comprehend it.

When the mules were loaded and being led away up the sandy slopes towards greener, more inviting surroundings, Ross joined them.

'We'll break the back of the journey before we stop for something to eat,' he said. 'Ready, Pastor? You'll have to ride the rest of the way. How about you, Miss Whitney, ever been on a horse before?'

'No, but I am sure I will manage,' Mary Kate assured him without revealing the momentary panic which touched her. On horseback until dusk! She would fall off from tiredness if from nothing else.

'Good, I'll leave you in Simon's capable hands then. Chin Ho has packed some cold food which will keep us going until we reach the house. Tonight we shall all eat well, I promise you. Mamalou's cooking is something special.'

'Who is Mamalou?' Mary Kate whispered as Simon helped her on to the back of a docile looking brown horse. He handed her the reins with a grin.

'The best cook this side of Boston, but don't tell Chin Ho I said so. Whenever the two of them meet there are fireworks, so they take turns to cook at the house now. Mamalou is Ross's housekeeper. She looked after him when he first came to Oahu. The old Captain, his father, brought her here from Honolulu and then married her, so in effect she's also his stepmother. They were only married native-style, under the *tapa* blanket, mind you, so there are some people who won't think it legal or binding. Ross's father did though. He loved that chunk of womanhood until the day he died. Ross feels the same way about her too. She's a mile wide, never stops laughing and she's my mother-in-law. Kiki is her daugher.'

Mary Kate felt her mouth gape. Ross's stepmother! Simon's mother-in-law! That made Kiki Ross's half-sister. And her sister-in-law! She stole a glance at her father as he mounted the horse a sailor held for him. He did not look too pleased at what he had heard. He had found more than a son! Would he recognise their existence? Oh, how could he ignore them, she thought, for they sounded such pleasant people and friendly. Above all, they were in sore need of friends in this new land.

The cavalcade moved off slowly towards the interior. With the sound of the sea behind them and the *Moonflower* riding at anchor on a calm sea, they proceeded at a leisurely pace as if there was all the time in the world to reach their destination. Thinking about it, Mary Kate realised that was true. There was no reason on earth to hurry and as the journey continued she found herself enthralled by the scenery.

She had found Honolulu interesting, but had never had the time to venture more than half a mile from the village. This new countryside did indeed herald the approach of paradise. Small, undulating hills rose out of the grasslands now that they had left the treeless flats which surrounded the village and the coarse *pili* grass had completely vanished. The grass here was thick and high, sometimes coming up to her thighs. The giant ferns grew more dense as did the tall trees with their foliage which sometimes entwined over the track they were following, to make an attractive arch of green, dappled with sunlight, where multi-coloured birds sang or watched curiously the progress of these intruders into their domain.

The deeper they went, the closer towards the mountains, the prettier she thought everything became. She heard the sound of running water a full five minutes before they came upon a crystal clear stream cascading from between some rocks into a small pool so clear she could see her reflection in it. Ross called a halt and Simon helped her to dismount. Her legs were so stiff he had to hold her until the circulation returned enabling her to walk. Immediately she found herself a place beside the water, running her fingers through the cold water and then dabbing them across her burning cheeks.

'Father, do come and sit here,' she said. 'I think Simon is bringing us some food. I'm starving, even though I ate such a large breakfast.'

She felt like a child again on her first visit to the circus, excited, bubbling over with enthusiasm for what lay ahead. She no longer feared it. She welcomed the challenge as she hoped he did.

'You are looking remarkably cheerful considering we have been perched on the back of some of the most uncomfortable creatures God ever put on this earth,' Nathaniel replied drily as he seated himself beside her. She looked different in a way he would not define at that moment. She had not wanted to come with him, he knew that, but she was duty-bound to obey him. She had resented him and his task ever since they left Boston, yet now she seemed to accept it. Simon, of course! She expected to lean on him, to use him as her crutch whenever there was ill feeling between them, as she had done when they were children. That was not going to be possible. Simon would follow in his footsteps as he had always been meant to do. If it was not the wish of God, why had he been brought to this den of iniquity so far from civilisation and found his son already here? It had been predestined. Who was he to question the working of a mind far above his limited intelligence? It was enough that he believed it had all been part of a special plan for him and his son. Once he was settled in the village of this high and mighty Prince he would talk to Simon, without his daughter's knowledge. She had always led him astray with her wilful ways. For all he knew she had instigated his leaving home in the first place.

Simon squatted on his heels beside them and offered them cold pieces of chicken which they both accepted. He had some wine in a goatskin sack, but only he drank any before he stretched out on the grass and folded his arms beneath his head.

'This is beautiful countryside, Simon,' Mary Kate said, her eyes glowing as she followed the flight of a honeycreeper, darting from branch to branch with an agility that took her breath away until he found a suitable perch where he could crack a nut between his beak. The heat had lessened as the afternoon lengthened and she was not so uncomfortable as when they first set out. Most of the men had their shirts wide open, sleeves rolled back. They lounged in the shade of the trees eating and drinking and making casual conversation. As usual the Princess Lani looked cool and elegant beneath the *kahili* which fanned her and kept at bay the numerous flying insects. 'How much further is it?'

Simon glanced briefly up at the sun before answering. 'Another two hours. Tired?'

'A little. And stiff. I've never been on a horse before.'

'You'll have plenty of time to get used to riding. Ross has a fine stable of horses. Kiki and I often go up into the mountains when I'm home, for a picnic.'

By the time Ross gave orders for everyone to remount, Mary Kate felt refreshed and rested. Fifteen minutes had had the same effect as an hour in such pleasant surroundings. As a child she remembered her mother often taking her and Simon to the park at least one afternoon a week. In the bag she carried would be freshly made lemonade, honeyed cakes she had baked herself that morning and sweets. They played games on the grass before they ate and Mary Kate also remembered she had never wanted to go back to the dull, cheerless house they lived in, to spend the remainder of the evening after dinner listening to her father reading from the Bible, often questioning them on parts of it and expecting their answers to be faultless.

Exactly as it was then, so it was now, she realised, with her in her mother's place. Already she had lost much of the wilfulness of her youth, she must not surrender the remainder. She was going to become a teacher. In that way she would be serving God as well as pleasing himself. Was that a sin? His word through her would be passed on to the children she taught, with love and affection, not threats and visions of dire consequences for failure to obey what was learned, as was her father's way.

They passed a strange looking object at one side of the track, several wooden sticks with a *tapa* folded over them and in front, in a bowl, what she could only surmise were some kind of offerings or gifts of leaves and fruit. As she lifted her eyes questioningly towards her brother, Ross, riding alongside her remarked quietly,

'Offerings to one of their gods. It's a kind of idol.'

It was the first time she had come across anything relating to the old religion that could be seen and touched. It looked so harmless.

'One day it will be replaced with a cross,' Nathaniel said loudly from behind and Ross gave a grimace as he looked back over his shoulder at the older man.

'Not in your time. Or mine. Don't try to change things too quickly, Pastor, or you will find yourself more involved with their gods than you wish to be.'

'That is why I am here.'

'I didn't quite mean it that way. Tamori is caught between the old and the new at the moment, harassed from all sides by those who want him to accept new ideas and others who threaten him with the vengeance of his gods if he does not keep to the old religion. Rather like your own faith in a way, isn't it? Behave—believe—or else!' With a sardonic smile twisting his lean mouth, he touched his hand to his cap in a sketchy salute in Mary Kate's direction and rode ahead to ride beside Tamori and his sister.

Simon threw an enquiring look at his sister, as if taken aback by his captain's attentions to her. She pretended not to notice. He was playing a game with her. It meant nothing to him—or to her—and she must not allow his sarcasm or his insufferable rudeness to penetrate her defences. She had more important things to think about than an overbearing man, without faith or scruples. What she felt whenever they came together was not attraction, she decided, but annoyance. She felt better having made up her mind to that. Annoyance—nothing more!

During the next two hours they passed more delightful little waterfalls cascading from rocky crevices, where creepers spread across the volcanic stone like a thick carpet and the air was heavy with the scent of stephanotis. Through little villages where people clustered to watch them pass. More than once a woman reached out to touch the hem of Mary Kate's skirts in wonderment. It was obvious they had never seen a white woman before. The conditions in which they lived looked terribly primitive. Most of them, men, women and children wore few clothes. Most wore nothing at all. The bodies of the men were more hideously tatooed than those she had seen in Honolulu. The designs which often covered all the exposed parts of their bodies were made with sharp-edged boned *adzes*, to which vegetable dyes were added to give a colourful, flamboyant finish. She shuddered at the thought of her skin being sliced with a sharp stone object and quickly averted her gaze.

The houses looked overcrowded, nearly every woman she saw had at least two children hovering about her, several had as many as five or six. The fields were cultivated, but poorly, as it there was no enthusiasm to raise crops for their own needs.

'These people are crying out for our help,' her father said, as distressed as she was at the sights they beheld. For once she was in complete agreement with him. Their motives differed, but their object was the same. To help these poor wretched creatures and give them a better way of life.

The way ahead began to slope downwards into a fertile valley where she could see large expanses of ground already cultivated. Men digging off to her left had cleared the land of trees and shrubs and were now turning the soil over in preparation for new crops. Overhead a kite wheeled and circled waiting anxiously for the movement of any small animal below on which he could feed. Was this the beginning of the plantation belonging to Ross Pendennis?

Her incredulity grew with each passing moment as her eyes saw fields of sweet potatoes and melons ripening in the sunshine. There were row upon row of orange and lemon trees, some bearing fruit, others covered in sweet-smelling blossom. A group of horses passed them watched over by two *kanakas* who greeted the captain as an old friend and satisfied her unasked question. There were pens where hogs, fat and succulent, awaited their call to the dinner table. Goats with their young, roamed free on the luscious grass which bordered the approach to the house, a track wide enough for two carts side by side to pass down without difficulty. The earth was hard and deeply rutted from the heavy traffic which had passed over it.

Still unbelieving of what they had come upon, she raised her eyes and looked ahead—and saw the house.

It lay at the end of the valley, the widest point, surrounded by smaller straw huts and storerooms, all bulging with grain and fruit, she noticed as they passed and there was an appetising aroma of beef coming from one of them which made her realise she was growing hungry again. How her appetite had sharpened in the keen mountain air.

The frame house itself, built of pine, was completely enclosed by palings, as many of the houses and shops in Honolulu had been, although she had seen nothing on such a grand scale as this. It was a house fit for a king! Was that how Ross Pendennis considered himself here?

Simon chuckled as he slipped his arms about her waist and assisted her to firm ground once more.

'Surprised? I thought you would like it.'

'It's very—grand.' It was the only word she could think of.

'Wait until you see the inside. Come on, let's bid farewell to the Prince and his sister and then I'll take you inside.'

'They are not staying here then?'

'Tamori like the comforts his wives have to offer. He left them behind this trip, so he will be in for some pampering when he gets home. Lani would like to, but Ross has never allowed it yet and I don't think he ever will. He goes to her when the need takes him.'

'Simon, do you have to be so crude?'

'It's a fact of life, my sweet little sister. One you will have to get used to if you are going to live here. It happens all the time and is as natural to the natives as breathing.'

'Captain Pendennis is not a native,' she insisted. 'Does he have no standards?'

'Strangely enough he does, which is why she does not share his bed here. This is his father's house. Mamalou and Kiki live here. His private life he keeps very private, believe me.'

As they aproached the spot where the Prince and Princess stood, Ross turned to greet them, his eyes lingering for a long moment on Mary Kate's flushed cheeks and bright eyes. A wispy red curl brushed one cheek, stirred by the wind, and she hastily strove to push it back behind her ears. How long would it last, he wondered, this pose of innocence?

'Welcome to my kingdom,' he said in a quiet tone.

She wished he had not chosen to use those exact words. Somehow it gave the impression that he was all-powerful and that, she found, was rather a frightening thought.

CHAPTER
FOUR

ALL BUT two of the *Moonshadow*'s crew left with Prince
Tamori and his sister, to go on to the village which
lay another mile beyond the boundaries of Ross
Pendennis's lands. With them went four well-laden
burros, only one of which belonged to the seamen. The
others held gifts for the royal pair. Bolts of cloth, Simon
told her, rare crystal and china from the East and richly
patterned carpets which Lani had specifically asked to be
brought back for her.

The Prince said a very cordial goodbye to Mary Kate
and her father, obviously well pleased with the presents
he had received, and said he would receive them in a few
days. In the mean time he would send a messenger to the
King with news of their arrival in his village. They would
have to abide by Kamehameha's reply. Mary Kate did
not miss the gleam which arose in the eyes of Kalakui at
the words and instinctively she knew he did not want
them to stay any more than did the beautiful woman at
his side.

As she watched the high priest help her to mount her
horse, she wondered if Lani was still the man's mistress
as well as that of Ross. There was something very
intimate in the way his hands lingered until the very last
moment on her body, the way his eyes held hers, the
smile she bestowed on him as she straightened once
again, and took the reins of the animal. Lani never likes

to discard anyone who may be useful to her, Simon had
said. She found herself wondering if Kalakui would
allow himself to be tossed aside, rejected by any woman,
even a princess. He did not look weak or easily led. He
was a powerful figure in his own right. He would be the
most difficult obstacle in their path.

'Goodbye, Your Highness.' Ross took his leave of
Tamori, showing no signs of the tiredness he felt. He
would never have admitted to anyone, especially the
female standing close by watching the scene from beneath veiled lids, but he had one hell of a hangover and
was looking forward to a hot tub and some of Mamalou's
good cooking to put him back in a good frame of mind.
He would need to be in a good humour to play host to his
two Bible-preaching guests. Ye gods! How would
he survive their sanctimonious twaddle? 'Goodbye,
Princess.'

She gave him a penetrating look, her full mouth
deepening into an inviting smile which brought instant
annoyance to Kalakui's eyes. How like Lani to enjoy
playing one man off against another. Thank God it
did not matter to him how many lovers she had. She
would destroy anyone stupid enough to really care for
her.

'I think you will be very bored before the evening is
out,' she purred softly. 'Come to me tonight. My company will be far more entertaining, I promise you.'

'Perhaps.' He was noncommittal as he stepped away
from her horse. As he did so, Kalakui jerked savagely on
the reins and the horse shied nervously. 'Gently, my
friend,' he added and the dark eyes held a warning the
other man could not fail to see—and understand. 'A
mare is like a woman, she must be led gently or she will
not follow you.'

'One day,' Simon said, stifling his laughter at the jibe, 'you will push him too far.'

'Then at least we will fight out in the open. I like it better that way. Let's get into the house. We are all tired and we need to relax. Hopi, unpack the mules and leave everything on the verandah for Mamalou to see. I can't wait to see her face. She'll have to clear half a dozen shelves to accommodate what I've brought this time. Still, I'll soothe her ruffled feathers with some Chinese silk and those embroidered fans I bought in Canton.'

He strode ahead of them towards the house. Simon tucked his sister's arm beneath his and she could feel the excitement in him as they followed. She looked at her father, but his expression betrayed nothing, not even relief that he was going to sleep in a comfortable bed tonight.

Mary Kate's expectations as to what she would find once she stepped over the threshold of the house, were fulfilled—and more. From the verandah where the *kanakas* were piling boxes galore, carpets and crates, they entered through a large pine door which gleamed in the late afternoon glow of sunshine. Soon it would be dark and her eyes immediately flew to the wrought iron candelabra which contained at least fifty candles. Ross Pendennis had described it as 'his kingdom'. Now she understood why there had been such pride in his voice. It did not stem from an egotistical sense of grandeur, although she sensed that here in this place that was his very own he would be complete master, but from something which went far deeper into the depths of him, into a part she had never touched. She wondered if anyone ever had. This was where he was happy, content, at peace with himself and the world. Here were his friends, Simon, his stepmother Mamalou, his half-sister Kiki and of course, Lani, whenever he chose to go to her. Would he go to her tonight as she had asked? She became aware of someone staring at her and lifted her eyes to meet those of Ross, jet pools, bottomless, unfathomable and yet for a moment, she was almost sure, he knew what had been in her mind. How ridiculous!

'You have done well for yourself, Captain,' Nathaniel said as he took in his new surroundings with hawk-like gaze. He missed nothing. The rich tapestries which hung from the pine walls, the heavily carpeted staircase leading to the upper part of the house. Glass in all the windows, crystal chandeliers, wealth shouting at him from every corner.

'God helps those who help themselves,' Ross returned solemnly. 'Hard work brings its own rewards, doesn't it, Pastor? My father built this place when Kamehameha gave him some land here in the valley. When he died, I extended it and at the moment I'm engaged on an interesting project which, to my knowledge, has never taken place in the islands before. I brought some pineapples back with me from one of my visits to your own country and now I have two quite flourishing acres of the things. I'm always interested in new ideas, new ventures, which will help my people.'

'Your people?' Mary Kate echoed and he turned to look at her with raised eyebrows as if he was surprised at the question.

'I've lived here for fifteen years, Miss Whitney. I consider this my home and these people, my people. Wouldn't you say that was being a true Christian? Isn't that why you and your father are here, to take these people to your bosoms, accept them as your brothers and sisters?' And change their way of life to one which they neither want nor will accept, he almost added, but catching Simon's eye he did not. He *was* tired. He was letting them get to him already!

At that moment something very large, clad in a robe of the most startling shade of blue Mary Kate had ever seen, materialised from a side-room and headed in Ross's direction.

'Ross! You are early. That no good *kanaka* said nightfall. Dinner is nowhere near ready.'

'Mamalou, it doesn't matter. You look good enough to eat right now.' Ross grabbed at the enormous woman, enveloping her in a bear hug which would have choked the breath from a strong man, yet appeared to do nothing for her, except make her convulse with laughter as he planted kisses on her cheeks and mouth.

Simon glanced at his sister in amusement. He had said a mile wide, she mused, and he was right. Beneath the flowing dress there must have been at least seventeen stone! Her brown hair was thick and wavy, pulled back into one long plait which hung down her back. She had a kind face, Mary Kate thought, affectionate, genuine. The eyes which turned in her direction as Ross released her showed only momentary surprise before they registered pleasure.

'You didn't say you were bringing a young lady.' Her English was near perfect with only a slight accent. 'I'll give her the little room that overlooks the garden.'

'This is Miss Mary Kate Whitney and Nathaniel Whitney, her father,' Ross said. 'They happen to be Simon's sister and father, so you'd better find Kiki and warn her to put on her prettiest dress to meet her new relatives.'

'That girl has been ready ever since you sent word of your coming,' Mamalou beamed in the direction of the two newcomers. Obviously she was used to having unexpected guests thrust upon her, Mary Kate thought as she smiled back. Nathaniel nodded, only just. He was not looking forward to seeing Simon's wife, she realised. Would he meet her? Accept her?

Simon caught her eye and she saw he was thinking along the same lines.

'Perhaps I'd better go and—prepare her for the great occasion. Mamalou, take care of my sister and father, will you? If they feel like I do, they'll be wanting a hot bath and a chance to rest awhile before dinner.'

He kissed Mary Kate on the cheek and left them.

'Which would you like first?' Ross asked, leading them into a large, well furnished room and indicating they should make themselves comfortable in the huge leather armchairs available. 'A bath, a rest or something to drink?'

'I would love something cool to drink,' Mary Kate replied without hesitation. 'After that ride I'm parched. And more than a little stiff. May I really have a bath?' To soak in the luxury of hot water was something she had not done since they arrived on Oahu. She had managed to find a quiet part of the beach where she could have a daily wash and sometimes a relaxing swim, without being observed, but her father had discovered what she was doing and forbidden her to do so again lest she be seen coming out of the water in only her wet shift.

'We are putting you to too much trouble, Captain,' Nathaniel intervened, but his objection was brushed aside.

'Nonsense. This is an open house, we are used to people coming and going at all hours of the day. When you've been here a little longer, Pastor, you will appreciate these small comforts, believe me. You will take coffee, or tea, or perhaps you prefer hot chocolate?'

'Coffee will be most appreciated, sir. I thank you.'

'Good. Mamalou, something cold for Miss Whitney, coffee for the Pastor and my usual. I'm parched too. Then make sure there are gallons of hot water for us all. After that we are going to descend on your cooking like ravenous animals.'

'Do you ever do anything else?' the woman laughed and waddled away to another room.

'You—live well, Captain. I have to admit, I did not expect anything like this,' Nathaniel remarked. He had been in a house like this only once before, the night he had asked for Maureen's hand in marriage and her father had laughed in his face and ordered him from the house before he set the dogs on him. His precious daughter, heiress to a fortune, marry a penniless Methodist preacher! She was being courted by the sons of titled landowners, with vast fortunes in their Irish purses. She would make a good marriage. Besides, she was a Catholic.

Nathaniel had begged, on his bended knees. He had been young then, full of high ideals, the fire of his faith that convinced him God was on his side in everything he did. He was more convinced of it when Maureen persuaded him they should elope. Once they were married, her father would relent and accept him. He would have his own parish, a fine house for them to raise their family. She even converted to his own faith, so great was her love for him.

And so they married, but her father did not change his mind. He disinherited her, refused her access to the house ever again, even to collect her clothes. Nathaniel found himself still penniless, with a wife to support, no future in that part of Ireland where Catholicism held sway and very soon there was also a baby on the way. Maureen had been happy to be with him alone. She never regretted what she had done, what she had given up for love. It took Nathaniel only three months to realise he had never loved her. Without the prospect of her father's money and powerful name behind them, she meant nothing to him and so, as they struggled to survive from day to day, he turned his anger and frustration on to the one person who truly loved him.

They used what little money they possessed to take passages aboard a cargo ship bound for America—a new life, the chance to become a man again. Their son was born on the ship. It seemed a good omen, but as the years passed, their status did not improve. Somehow Nathaniel never found himself able to communicate with the people who came to him in need, for his help, his words of comfort. All he could give them were the words he lived by, the words of the Bible. Uncompromising, unrelenting. The laws of God.

Now he had come full circle. Ross Pendennis stood in the place of Maureen's father, wealthy, proud, arrogant, breaking commandment after commandment in his desire for pleasure. Now Nathaniel knew at last why he had disliked him on first sight. Here was the devil he had to destroy before he could reach anyone else. But he would have to move carefully, slowly, so that the man suspected nothing. This time he would not fail!

'What is it, Father? Are you feeling unwell?' Mary Kate was looking at him anxiously. He looked so strange.

'On the contrary, I am feeling better than I have felt in months.'

Mamalou brought in a tray with a jug of fruit juice on it, coffee and a decanter of whisky which Ross reached for with a nod of appreciation. He noticed the best glasses were being used and the china coffee set usually reserved for visiting dignitaries like Tamori or Kamehameha's tax collector. Mamalou ignored his pointed gaze, enquired if there was anything else and when he shook his head, left them saying she would go and see to rooms for their guests. There was enough hot water for one bath now, she told them, the rest would be ready in half an hour.

A shaggy dog came flying through the door as Mary Kate was finishing her second glass of fruit juice and launched himself at Ross. Huge paws fastened on his shoulders and a wet tongue subjected him to soggy kisses for several minutes. He did not appear to mind it in the least.

'Glad to see me, boy? I'm glad to be home too. Where have you been, the river again?' He was looking at the wet paw marks which led from the door to his chair. 'Fishing, eh? Where's Kiki? Go and find her and bring her here. Go on.'

'He's very affectionate,' Mary Kate said, her eyes brimming with amusement. She and Simon had never been allowed to have a pet of their own.

'I dragged him out of the harbour in Honolulu when he was a pup. Someone had thrown him overboard.'

'How cruel.'

'That's life. Even paradise has its moments of cruelty.'

It sounded almost like a warning, she thought apprehensively. Against what?

'You take the first hot water.' Ross rose to his feet. 'I'll show you to your rooms, your luggage should be unpacked by now. The bathroom is between them. Primitive by Boston standards you may find, but not by those of the islands.'

'You are being very kind, Captain, we do appreciate it,' Mary Kate said as she rose.

'After the deplorable conditions you were living in before I think you both deserve the comforts of home,' he returned lightly.

They followed him up the pine staircase with its ornate carved handrail, to a corridor where the polished wood floors were covered with oriental mats of varying designs and colours. A ship's wheel hung from one of the walls, a painting of a schooner from another. His father's ship, Mary Kate wondered? The one he had sold in order to buy the *Moonflower*. She must remember to ask him about that name, it intrigued her.

Her father was shown to his room, she to hers, several doors further on. Her meagre belongings had been unpacked and were lying across a chair. She felt acute embarrassment to know Ross saw them. Old clothes, worn shoes. Nothing new or pretty. How much she wanted to be like other girls of her age, go to parties on the arm of an eligible young man who would whisper sweet compliments in her ear and dance with her until the early hours of the morning. As her mother had done. When she had been little and unable to sleep, her mother would creep into bed beside her and tell her of her own childhood among the rolling hills of Ireland. The big house where she had been born and raised, the lavish balls she had been to with her parents, her clothes and jewels. At times like those, her mother had become young again, her eyes, as blue as her daughter's, would shine with excitement, the pleasure of memories, which were all that were left to her now.

And lost to Mary Kate. She thought she had accepted it, put all thoughts to the back of her mind once they arrived in Honolulu, but the sight of this house had revived all those stories of grandeur and high living. Somewhere in Ireland she had a grandfather who was rich and powerful, but her father would never speak of him. He could have given them all they needed if a reconciliation had come about, as it well might if she had been able to meet him. Or so she told herself, during those long, dark nights when she had gone to bed hungry because the food was scarce, cold because there were not enough blankets for the bed. Dreams. That was all she had ever had. Did God not care how her mother had suffered? How poor she and her father were? She reproved herself instantly for such sinful thoughts. Of course He did. Had He not guided their footsteps to this island to find Simon again?

The bedroom was small, but pleasantly furnished with pretty covers on the bed and at the dressing-table. Matching drapes hung at the window which looked out on to a well-tended garden. She could smell the heady scent of night blooming flowers wafting into the room. As tantalising as the most expensive perfume.

'I hope you will find this comfortable,' Ross said before he left her.

The moment the door had closed behind him she flung herself across the bed, gasping at its softness. A real feather mattress! What luxury. The temptation to close her eyes and sleep had to be fought off and with great reluctance she got up again and began to put her clothes away in the closet. There was a large mirror on the front of the door and she gazed at her reflection in dismay. The sun had reddened her cheeks and her hair was in disarray. What a sight she looked! She picked up the dress she had left across the bed, a dark green cotton, edged with white lace—her best!—and went to find the

bathroom so that she could make herself more presentable to go down to dinner.

She caught her breath in sheer delight as she opened
the door and stepped into the bathroom. All the walls
were tiled—an oriental design again. A large blue and
white tub stood in the corner of the room, together with
a dainty porcelain hand basin on a white stand. There
were coloured towels hanging from a rail. Tentatively
she tested the water which filled the bath almost to the
brim. It was just right. She wasted no time in undressing
and sinking into it, soaping herself vigorously until she
was lathered from head to toe. How she prayed her
father would not be too anxious to leave the hospitality
Ross Pendennis was offering them.

Minutes later Mamalou's head appeared around the
door enquiring if she required more hot water. Mary
Kate resisted the temptation to say yes, remembering
there were other tired bodies longing for the tub too.
With great reluctance she climbed out and dried herself,
rubbing her skin until it glowed. She twisted her damp
hair into its usual tight knot and then pulled on the green
dress and clean stockings.

As she emerged from the bathroom and turned back
towards her room, her attention was caught by the
delicate glow of candlelight from a room at the end of the
corridor. Through the open door she could see walls
lined with bookshelves, large pieces of heavy, ornate
furniture gleaming in the muted light and curiosity took
her footsteps beyond the door of her own room to the
threshold of the other. It was the most beautiful room
she had ever seen in her life. In it Ross Pendennis had
placed objects from voyages all around the world, she
suspected, although she could not begin to guess the
origins of the exquisite jade statuettes which had the

place of honour against the far wall, or the magnificent carpet beneath her feet, or the savage-looking weapons on another wall. There were brass ornaments and fragile glass which took away her breath with the intricacy of design, and filigree silver, alongside silver tankards and plates on an enormous dresser which must have been at least six feet in length.

Her gaze fastened on a painting suspended over a small window. It was the *Moonflower*. The figurehead of a woman with blazing red hair streaming past bare shoulders startled her. She had not taken much notice of it before.

'It's meant to be the goddess Pele—their fire-goddess,' Ross remarked from the armchair where he had been watching her since she entered the room. 'Tamori had it carved for me when I bought the ship.'

Mary Kate wheeled around to face him with a gasp of dismay. He was almost lost in the huge chair despite his height and build and she had passed him by without realising his presence.

'I'm sorry. I—I was curious. The room looked so—inviting.'

'That's the first time I've ever heard it described that way by anyone other than myself.' He rose to his feet, stubbing out the ash of a long cigar in a glass tray on the table beside him. 'This is my—inner sanctum.'

'Then I will go at once. I did not mean to intrude.'

'Don't be silly. Why do you find it inviting, Miss Whitney?'

She watched him cross to a decanter and glasses on a pewter tray and pour wine for them both.

'Not for me.' Her words fell on deaf ears. He came back to where she stood and held out a glass to her.

'You enjoyed it the other night. It's Duncan's punch.

He brings me a couple of cases every trip here. You haven't answered my question.'

She took the glass. What else could she do, but make a scene like a silly schoolgirl and refuse it. She ignored the smile which crossed his face as she drank a little before answering.

'It is . . . it offers warmth and comfort from the outside world. Does that sound naive? I think this is your special place because you can come here when you are troubled and your mind will be soothed. Come here when you are happy and gain more pleasure from the things you have put here. And just come and sit and enjoy what you own.'

'You have gained more pleasure from this room than anyone else who has been in it,' Ross said and there was a strange light flickering in the depths of his eyes as he turned away to refill his empty glass. 'Many of these things I brought back when my father was alive and we sailed together. It brings me close to him to see them again.'

'And your mother?' Mary Kate asked. There was no sign as far as she could see of any presence, other than that of Mamalou, in the house.

'She did not come with us to the islands.' For a moment the handsome face was dark with thoughts she knew nothing about and the look troubled her. It was almost murderous. Instinctively she knew it was time to change the subject. Unwittingly she had stumbled on to a forbidden topic.

'You have a very beautiful house, Captain. Truly beautiful. How lucky you are to have been to all those far away places and gathered such treasures. You have the wealth in knowledge and skill, of so many cultures different from our own. If I was a man I would travel too . . .' She broke off, her cheeks flooding with colour as if she thought she had spoken too freely. He had that effect on her. There were moments like this, when she was at ease with him, also many when she was not. These were so much more enjoyable.

She was beautiful, Ross thought experiencing sudden shock waves pulsating through his body. He watched her move to examine a jade statuette he had brought back from his last voyage and the candlelight enhanced the fiery tresses even though they were in that abominably uninteresting knot at the nape of her neck, slanted across her face, revealing an exquisiteness of bone structure he had not noticed before. Why had he ever thought her plain? Dull?

She was as unaware of his scrutiny as she was of her own potential, he realised. As yet life with all its disturbing implications had not touched her. With a Bible-thumping tyrant full of his own self-righteous importance ruling her life, it was little wonder. He would have ruled her life from the moment she entered the world and would seek to control it until the day she died.

He had a rival now. The islands had a way of reaching out to claim unsuspecting hearts. He ought to know. His own father had been a victim and he himself had tried to leave a dozen times after his death, only to return time and time again to the place he knew as home, drawn back by an irresistible spell which had been woven about him as a child. He belonged here. He would always stay.

Ross's eyes came back to Mary Kate's face. Innocence and beauty. He believed in neither in a woman. Perhaps she had not been exposed long enough to the world for it to corrupt her, but it would not take long. One man telling her how lovely she was, one man willing to give up his soul to have her and she would realise the power at her fingertips and then, like all women, she would use it.

'Why do you wear your hair in such an unbecoming fashion?' he asked boldly and before Mary Kate could guess his intentions, he had put down his glass, taken her by the shoulders and guided her to a wall mirror. His fingers removed the two tortoiseshell combs which held it securely in place before he stepped back. The long tresses tumbled past her shoulders like tongues of deep red fire and words of protest died unuttered on her lips as she felt him lift strands of it between his fingers and lay them gently about her cheeks. Quickly she put down her glass, her hand was trembling so much she was afraid she would drop it. 'That's better. Much, much better. It's soft, like silk. Don't you agree it's an improvement?'

She gazed at the new image. She looked—pretty! Framed by the loose tresses, her face had lost that pointed look she hated.

'I—I don't know.'

'Liar,' he mocked. 'Tell me, Mary Kate, has your father ever allowed any man to come as close to you as I am now? Has there ever been a single instant when you evaded his eagle eye and sought solace with some young man?'

Mary Kate spun around with a gasp, outraged by such an audacious suggestion and found his dark eyes were gleaming wickedly. He was everything she had been brought up to detest. He drank to excess from what she had seen at the *luau* in Honolulu, consorted with loose women without shame or conscience. Worst of all, he mocked her faith. Was it possible he sensed it was not as strong as it had once been and sought to destroy it totally by flagrantly displaying these things before her?

He was everything she hated and yet she found him attractive. How could that be so? How could she want to

feel those lips touching hers, his arms holding her close?
His taunt had unknowingly wounded her deeply for no
man had ever held her in love—nor so much as kissed
her!

Love and hate bound together as one emotion? It was
not possible. Why had she thought of love? She had
never known it. When she did it certainly would not be
for a man like Ross Pendennis. He would use her for a
moment's pleasure and then discard her—if she allowed
it.

How those eyes suddenly blazed with frightening
passion. She knew he was going to kiss her and panic
seized her. She tried to push past him, but he caught her
up in his arms. Her fists pounded against his chest, but he
held her fast against him and was too strong for her to
break free. Her eyes dilated with horror as his mouth
descended on hers, shutting off a cry.

She had always imagined the first time she was kissed
would be something to remember for the rest of her life.
A moment of great importance to be treasured. It was
not like that at all. The illusion was brutally shattered as
Ross' mouth bruised her soft lips. There was no gentleness! He gave nothing! He took with a ruthless force
which sought to make her submit to his domination.

She closed her eyes, submitting to the tortuous moment which seemed to go on for ever. He never knew the
effort it cost her. When he released her she was trembling from head to toe and huge tears were brimming in
her blue eyes.

'Now I know the face of the devil.' Her voice shook
too, but whether it was from outraged indignation or the
fear of what he had aroused in her, she did not know.

'It's what you wanted. I saw it on your face when you
looked in the mirror,' Ross chuckled sardonically.

'You're not trying to tell me you haven't been kissed before. I admit you could do with a little more practice. Come on, admit you liked it.'

'You—you are beneath contempt.' The tears could not be contained and spilled down over chalk-white cheeks. They only served to further his amusement.

'Good God, girl! If you don't want to dance with the devil, you shouldn't call on him in the first place.' He suddenly realised he was angry with himself and did not understand why. He had kissed dozens of women without ever feeling as if he had committed some heinous crime, as he did now. 'You are a child playing at being a woman. Go away, you begin to bore me.'

She fled from his tormenting presence without another word. Ross selected another cigar from the humidor on his desk, and lighted it in a thoughtful silence.

'Am I interrupting anything?' Simon asked from the doorway.

'Why should you think that? Come in and have a drink.'

'No, I'm still trying to persuade Kiki to come down to dinner. She's terrified of meeting Mary Kate and Father.' Simon's brows were drawn together into a deep frown as he stared at Ross. In the end he could contain the words no longer. 'I saw Mary Kate rush into her room as if a thousand devils were after her. I wondered if she had been quarrelling with Father again.'

Not a thousand devils, Ross thought, remembering that moment when he had felt her body respond to the caress of his hands. Just one! The fire was in her, waiting to be released. She was no different from all the rest.

'We were talking in here,' he said casually. Best to be honest about it before she ran to Simon with some wild story that he had tried to assail her non-existent virtue.

'Talking?'

'I kissed her. It was an impulsive gesture on my part.
I've never kissed a preacher's daughter before and she's
a damned pretty one. She wasn't exactly unwilling,' he
added as if in defence of his actions. Impulsive or not.

'Impulsive? Like the one to Tamori? You asked his
permission for them to come here, didn't you?' Simon
did not know whether to be angry or pleased by the
statement. A man like Ross could give his sister everything she wanted. Take her away from his father to a new
and exciting life. But he should have gone about it more
carefully. Mary Kate was not one of his waterfront
women. She did not go in for furtive kisses in dark
corners. God, he had not realised how inhibited their
lives had been until he left home. Now he knew things he
would never want her to know, had been to places he
would never speak of in her presence, had mixed with
the dregs of the earth in various ports, and come out
older and wiser for it. And he had found a woman to
make him happy. His sister was still innocent and un-
awakened, unprepared for the real world which might
force itself upon her at any time. He would have to have
a brotherly word with her—and soon.

'I thought you wanted your sister around for a while.
If Kamehameha turns down Tamori's request there will
be nothing I can do about it. A few weeks are better than
nothing, aren't they?' Ross asked, with a shrug of his
shoulders, intended to indicate his intervention was of
no great importance. 'Believe me, I have no interest in
her whatsoever. Does that set your mind at rest? Now go
and deal with that awkward wife of yours while I bathe
and change. Dinner will be ready before we are.'

*   *   *

Mamalou had set dinner out on a long table on the verandah, beneath sweet-smelling night flowers which entwined themselves in and out of the bamboo roof and filled the air with their heady perfume. She had put out the best china again, Ross noticed, and changed into her new *tapa* in honour of their guests. He had carefully avoided the kitchen as he came downstairs and heard Chin Ho's voice raised in protest. If just once they could combine to cook a meal it would be fit for a king, he decided. As it was, the one which arrived more than did justice to their appetites.

To start with there was fresh melon. That was followed by chicken coated in a thick, sweet sauce and served with bean sprouts and potatoes. The wily old fox had actually persuaded Mamalou to let him do the cooking, Ross mused as he tucked enthusiastically into the food placed in front of him. Afterwards there was fruit, piled high on a plate like a volcano.

Mary Kate was conscious, with every mouthful she took, of the man sitting at the head of the table. She dared not look in that direction and turned instead for conversation to Simon and his delightful little wife, Kiki. She was a pretty girl, rather on the plump side as were most of the island women she had seen. She had been quite embarrassed to discover she was regarded as 'painfully thin' and therefore would not catch the eye of a prospective husband. If she continued to eat as she was doing now, she would be the size of Mamalou!

Kiki was short for Kikioewa. Simon had fallen in love with her the first time Ross brought him to the house, he confessed. They were very much in love, Mary Kate decided, watching the secret glances they had for one another, the way his hand touched hers as if by accident, on so many occasions. So different from the rough, ungentlemanly fashion in which she had been treated earlier. And he had had the nerve to suggest she had wanted to be kissed. She had! She could not deny it to herself, although she would have died before admitting it to anyone else. He had seen it in her eyes and taken advantage of the moment. The fault had been as much hers as his. She would ensure it did not happen again.

Nathaniel was seated on her left. He had eaten well, but had taken little or no part in the conversation which flowed about the table. Kiki was ignored. He had not spoken to her since Simon had introduced her before the meal.

Mary Kate had felt so sorry for the girl and her brother too. They were being so patient. This was, after all, their home and her father was a guest. She was beginning to give up all hopes of a reconciliation between them, yet at one time, it was so close. One little show of need, of affection could have broken down the barriers forever and made them a complete family again. It hurt her deeply to see them divided, so distant, and for Kiki to feel an unwanted stranger beside her own husband.

'Tamori is sending word to the King about you tomorrow,' Ross said, looking down the length of the table to where Nathaniel sat. 'It may be some time before we hear anything in return, so I suggest you remain here until we know what is to happen to you. There is plenty of room here and it will give you a chance to get acquainted with the villagers. Simon can introduce you, show you around so that they get used to seeing you. If all goes well and Kamehameha allows you to remain, I've been thinking I may be able to help with some kind of accommodation for your schoolhouse. It's only a storeroom, but it has four walls and a roof. It's yours if you want it. You can always have some of my *kanakas* to help you with the work.'

'How generous. I regret, however, we must refuse the offer of charity, Captain. We will live in the village itself. I am sure we will find something suitable for our humble style of living. The storehouse, however, will be invaluable to us and we thank you for that. Unlike you, I do not think God has guided our footsteps here to have the King turn us away. He will give his permission. He will be guided by a higher force,' Nathaniel replied calmly.

He included his daughter in his speech and in his thoughts, Ross realised, yet at the same time he suspected she was never consulted over anything, however trivial, and by the dismayed look on her face, quickly veiled as her father turned to look at her, he knew she was deeply disappointed. Perhaps he had achieved more with one kiss than he had realised.

'The storehouse does have an adjoining dwelling,' Ross continued slowly. 'But it is hardly suitable for you—or your daughter. It hasn't been used for years. There are animals living in the rooms.'

The flint grey eyes which studied him indicated Nathaniel had taken his meaning and as they looked away again, ignored it.

'We are here to do God's will, Captain. His son was a humble carpenter, should His servants live better than He did?'

'Must they suffer unnecessarily too?' Ross flung back stubbornly. 'For heaven's sake, man. The conditions outside this house are more primitive than you can ever imagine. Honolulu gave you comforts you will never have here. They may have been few, but they were available. These mountain villages are not renowned for their enlightenment.'

'That is why we are here, is it not? To bring the Light of Truth into their lives? Your concern for my daughter's welfare is unnecessary. She is a strong girl, obedient and God fearing. She has not come all this way to turn her back on all she holds sacred.'

'Father,' Mary Kate protested quietly. 'I am sure the Captain meant well, he just does not understand that his needs are not ours.' She was aware of the surprise which leapt to her father's eyes. He would never have expected her to want to leave the comforts they had been offered, but then he did not know how much she wanted to get away from the man who had made the offer. The face of the devil was how she had described him. The destroyer of her soul, if she allowed it. Gathering all her courage she lifted her eyes to look at him, hating the smile which played around his mouth. 'Your offer was most kind, Captain, but I agree with my father. We will be better off in the village. Perhaps in time we will grow close to the people. It is all we ask.'

'I could help . . .' Kiki began tentatively and Mary Kate smiled gratefully. She caught Simon's nod of approval.

'I accept for us both. Please will you teach me your language first?'

'I will be your teacher as Ross was mine. We will learn from each other.' The girl looked relieved her offer was not rejected.

Mary Kate had taken the first step towards reuniting the whole family, and that included Kiki. She was part of it now. She felt suddenly elated. It was to occupy her mind in the days to come, helping to shut out the memory of Ross Pendennis watching her with his black panther's eyes.

'Perhaps you would take care of the arrangements in

the morning, Simon,' Ross suggested, nodding thanks as
Mamalou placed a third cup of coffee before him. He
had drunk too much wine and whisky, he realised, but
the hot stimulant was quickly restoring his faculties. It
was not a long ride to the village, but he knew he must be
alert and watchful as always lest one of Kalakui's as-
sassins was waiting for him in the darkness. The man
hated him for his possession of Lani, his friendship with
Tamori who he tried so hard to dominate and failed
because of Ross's guidance. The link had been forged
since childhood when he and Tamori and Lani had come
together and become friends to learn each other's ways
and language. Strangers for a short time only. Tamori,
Ross knew from past experience, was weak and easily
led, an easy target for the high priests who had ruled
their lives and those of the *kanakas* for countless years.
His friend would listen to the new ways, given time.
Approached with a velvet glove, not the iron fist wielded
by the fiery Nathaniel Whitney. The latter did not
inspire confidence, but fear. That was here already!

Ross wanted change. He abhorred the old ways, the
needless cruelty and slaughter, the absolute rule of one
man, in this case, Kamehameha, over so many ordinary
people. His English blood rebelled at such oppression,
but he stood it and lived with it, because it was not
possible for him alone to change it. But by being there
with Tamori, having access to the King and his ministers,
by being accepted, one day it would be possible that a
new generation would rise up and rebel, sweep away the
old laws, give wealth and prosperity and peace of mind
to a people well deserving of it in his opinion.

'Of course.' Simon seized the opportunity eagerly. He
liked the way Kiki and his sister had become immediate
friends. He never for one moment considered his

father's feelings. His arrival on Oahu had been an unpleasant shock, but he had absorbed it into a part of his mind that sheltered him from all unpleasantness. Many memories of his childhood were there in those dark recesses. Unwanted, unbidden into his new life.

'The place is a pest-hole, but you realise that anyway,' Ross continued. 'Take some men and see what you can do to clean it up quickly. Anything you need you will probably find here. Make the place habitable for human beings, however humble. I won't be back tonight, I'll probably see you sometime after midday.'

'You are going to that woman,' Nathaniel declared stonily. 'Is there nothing I can say to dissuade you?'

Across the flame of the match Ross was holding beneath his cigar, his eyes were suddenly like chips of granite. Mary Kate held her breath, casting an apprehensive glance at her brother who sat as if turned to stone by the statement.

'In this house we do not question each other's comings and goings, Pastor. We live our lives as we choose.'

'Outside the laws of God.'

'You are a guest in this house, Father,' Simon's voice was harsh with anger.

'It doesn't matter, Simon. Leave it,' Ross said in a quiet tone. 'In answer to your question. I would hate to disappoint you. Yes, I am going to her.'

'Then I will pray for your immortal soul.'

'Save your prayers for someone more worthy—or in need of them.' There was an infuriatingly mocking smile on Ross's face as he answered. 'I am neither. Don't you understand, I live my life the way I do because I enjoy it? I won't change it for man, woman or God.'

'Then your soul is surely damned.' He had been right, Nathaniel thought. Here was the true evil he was meant to combat. The natives were children, easily led by heartless, lusting men like this one who corrupted all those he came in contact with.

'It was, long before you came here. I believe everyone goes to hell in their own fashion and somewhere along the way they enjoy themselves. I'm heading straight for perdition and I don't give a damn, so don't waste your time on me.'

CHAPTER
FIVE

Mary Kate did not see Ross the next day. In fact it was three weeks before she set eyes on him again. Three weeks of back-breaking toil from dawn to dusk to turn the four rooms they had been given into a home.

The sight of the wild hogs running through the rooms, the dirt on the floors, the broken boxes piled high in one corner, did not daunt her in the least. It was no worse than the accommodation they had taken over in Honolulu and four rooms were better than one. And the help she received was heartwarming.

The village was an hour's ride from the house. They travelled there in two wagons. One carrying Simon, her father, Kiki and herself. The other was piled high with oddments of furniture which Simon had already loaded before anyone else was about, driven by a *kanaka* from the plantation, with another two men and two women seated somewhat precariously on top of the items. There was a dressing-table and two rocking chairs. A chest of drawers and a bookcase. Two brass bedsteads with feather mattresses and enough china and cooking utensils to set up house for a family of ten. There was also an antiquated iron stove. Mary Kate could have wept when she saw it. She had become very adept at cooking over an open fire outside, but she did not like it. Now she could make a real kitchen, bake bread and cakes again, nourishing meals. Perhaps even invite people to dinner as they became more settled.

Even Nathaniel, to everyone's surprise, took off his coat and climbed on to the roof with the *kanakas* to inspect the thick straw for damage, while Kiki and Mary Kate set to inside with brooms, coughing and choking at the clouds of dust they made with their vigorous sweeping. It took an hour for the dust to settle, during which time they took a well-earned rest before unloading the furniture, but by that time, the family of hogs had returned together with a dozen or more chickens who drove everyone wild as they attempted unsuccessfully to evict them. It was both funny and frustrating to see the *kanakas* rolling about on the ground, the tail of a baby hog or a chicken's leg in their grasp. As quickly as they tossed them out, they returned, for the house had no door and the paling surrounding it was broken in many places.

That night, after Simon and the others had gone home, Mary Kate cooked the chicken he had provided, one she suspected, which had not got away. As they ate beside the wagon, a woman brought them a jug of fresh goat's milk and some kind of biscuit. Mary Kate thanked her, knowing full well she did not understand a word. Curious eyes had been watching them all day. Some villagers came forward openly to offer help, others stood in the background, the sullenness of their expressions betraying the fact they did not approve of the white faces which had arrived in their midst. Neither approved, nor wanted, she suspected and was extra grateful for this simple act of kindness.

She pulled one of the feather mattresses from the wagon and made up a bed for her father beneath some shady trees, leaving the other where it was for herself. It was no use trying to move anything into the house until the fence was mended and all animals shut out.

She lay on her back beneath the stars and wondered how many eyes were watching them from the darkness. It was strange, but she felt no fear. In fact she felt very contented as she closed her eyes and drifted into a peaceful, well-deserved sleep.

Simon returned with the wagon bright and early next morning. The sound of hammering awoke her and she sat up, startled, to find he already had a door in place and Kiki was preparing a breakfast of eggs and ham which she had brought from the house. On the orders of Mamalou, Mary Kate was told when she tried to protest. She thought the *haolewahine* needed more meat on her bones to make her an attractive woman. Simon promptly folded with laughter at the comment and was chased from the scene by a red-faced sister wielding a broom, but he returned in time to sample his wife's cooking and voice his appreciation before he began work on the fence with the aid of the men he had again brought.

Without them they would have been helpless, Mary Kate thought with a rush of gratitude she found she could not put into words. She must redouble her efforts to bring them all together—and that included Kiki. Her father's improved attitude might open the way for her. He was being quite friendly with the *kanakas* and doing his fair share of the work. In his way, he was content too.

By the end of the week, the four bare rooms had undergone a major transformation. Swept clean with small carpets on the floors, furniture made new and bright with fresh coats of paint, doors on all the rooms to make them private from each other and the old stove, freshly blacked and now in working order, it was a home.

'Father,' Mary Kate touched Nathaniel on the arm as Simon and Kiki took their leave that last day. She—no, *they* owed them so much, they had to show their appreciation and gratitude. 'I would like to cook dinner for Simon tomorrow. May I? It would be so nice for us all to sit down together again. Our first meal in our new home.'

'That sounds like an excellent idea.' To her surprise he nodded approval. 'He is always welcome here, he knows that.'

'Simon, did you hear . . .' she began excitedly, only to have her father cut her short, with words that squashed all her hopes of reconciliation.

'Provided he comes alone. I will not have that woman in this house again.'

'You—you can't mean that?' she stammered in horror. The look of rejection on Kiki's face was too awful to bear. For three days he had been almost civil to her. 'She is Simon's wife.'

'His woman. That is a different matter. I have made my decision. You will abide by it, daughter.'

'You didn't really think he would change, did you?' Simon asked, with a harsh laugh. 'Don't you know by now how he uses people? You, me—our mother? He cares for no one. Even his so-called faith in God is a lie. It's a crutch because he's afraid of life. Don't you see that? He'll use anyone, anything. Destroy them! He'll destroy you in time.'

Mary Kate ran to him, took his face in her hands and pressed her lips to his cheeks. Then she embraced Kiki, uncaring that her father was watching. He was no Christian to turn his back on this girl. She could not understand it.

'Give me a little time,' she pleaded. 'He has been so different these past few days. Maybe he is changing. Dear Simon, Kiki, my dearest wish is for us to be a family. I pray for it each night. I will work for it, I promise. He will accept the love you have for each other in time.'

'Do you?' Simon asked tersely.

'Such love is to be envied,' Mary Kate said softly, truthfully, and he drew her into his arms with an oath.

'You and I must talk very soon. I have much to tell you. Why don't you come back with us? Let him live here alone. A little solitude might make him realise that the evil he seeks in others stems from within himself.'

'Don't talk like that. You don't understand.'

'It is you who does not understand, Mary Kate. No, you will not come, I can see that in your face. Then take care. For your own safety allow him to do nothing until Tamori hears from Kamehameha. He must not approach the villagers. Is that clear?'

'I will tell him. I do not think for one moment he will listen to me. He seems stirred with new fire. You should have heard him talk last night after dinner. The things we could do here, Simon. So much good. A school. A church. Is that so wrong?'

'My poor, sweet, innocent little sister, what am I going to do with you?' Simon gave her a swift hug before he put her from him and lifted Kiki into the wagon. 'I will be back in a few days, but not here. Meet me on Thursday at the Chandler's, down what we laughingly call a street here. It's off yonder into those trees. You'll find most things there that you will need and don't worry about running out of money. Ross owns the place as well as the trading store.'

'I would not like to owe money to the Captain,' Mary Kate said.

'What is a little money between friends, besides I will always cover it for you. If it wasn't for him you wouldn't have a roof over your head or a bed to sleep on, or plates to eat off. Who on earth do you think provided everything?'

'I—I thought you did.' She was aghast at the news. Ross Pendennis was their benefactor?

'Well now you know different,' her brother returned. '*Aloha*, Mary Kate. May all your dreams be pleasant ones.'

Dreams and hopes and flights of fancy were for children only, Mary Kate thought sadly as she watched them drive away. There was no room in her life for such things.

She saw Simon that Thursday and several times after that by prearrangement. Sometimes on the grassy slopes behind the village when he would bring Kiki, other times seemingly by accident in the local stores, almost all of which appeared to be owned by Ross Pendennis. Her father's comments when he learned of this were most scathing. His influence was as bad as that of the high priests, he declared. He had set himself above other men in the midst of simple-minded people who turned to him for help and guidance, little realising he only gave in order to control their minds, their lives.

The comparison Mary Kate drew was not a favourable one. It was almost a self-portrait. Was Simon right? Had he buried himself in his faith over the years afraid to face reality? The rejection by his father-in-law, the poverty which had followed, his failure to communicate to those people who had turned to him in need? In his determination to succeed, would he cast aside those he loved after their usefulness was over, reject out of hand love when it was offered? How could he refuse to acknowledge Kiki, whose love for his son shone from her eyes whenever she looked at him or his name was mentioned. They had discovered something beautiful, something to be cherished.

And yet, if her father had never known love . . . It was a chilling thought. If he had never loved her mother, only the wealth and position her family name would have brought him, then Simon had unknowingly shown her the answer. The one failure her father could not forgive himself for, the reason he rejected all attempts to reach him, to love him. He could not love! He could not give himself totally to one person. He had never known the bitter-sweet, tender moments shared with the one woman with whom he wanted to spend the rest of his life. He had never known passion, could not comprehend its promises, its pitfalls, the raptures of fulfilment. He had sought God as a sanctuary from that which he could not understand—or could not obtain, using Him as a shield.

The realisation stunned her for several days, but at the same time it made her understand so many things which had puzzled her before. Her mother's undying loyalty through all the hardships and painful labours which had befallen her, and she, the daughter of a titled Irish aristocrat, unused to any task lower than summoning a servant.

He will destroy you too, her brother had warned. She was forewarned now. She would not allow that to happen. She understood the ghost that haunted her father. In a way, she pitied him the things he had never known and prayed that the faith he had chosen to sustain him would prove strong enough if a formidable challenge ever arose.

The storeroom which adjoined the house, although not in a bad state of repair, did need a great deal of work done on it before Mary Kate considered it possible to put the idea of a school to Tamori. This, she had decided, should be approached as a totally different project, by her, not her father. The village was small and screamed of poverty, so different from Honolulu which she had found surprisingly prosperous, probably due to the trade from passing ships. But Wameia was nothing like that. The mud and straw, windowless huts were like those she had seen *en route* to Ross's house. The people, although they looked well-fed, had no interest in cultivating the lush greenery about them as the *kanakas* had done less than two miles away, turning bush and jungle into fertile, productive land where melons, oranges and other fruits ripened in the warm sun. The children played in the dust apparently content, as were their parents, with a way of life that demanded very little from them. But three weeks was so short a time. She had to be patient and await a message from the King. She dared not think of a refusal. What would they do? Where would they go? She began to realise how attached she had become to this primitive island paradise. She did not want to leave! She had found a delightful spot while walking one day, which she considered to be her own special place where she could go to be alone with her thoughts. The path she had followed had led her to a small pool, almost hidden among dense trees and ferns. A little bit of paradise had become hers, she thought, as she sat beside the pool and trailed her fingers in the cool water. Flowers grew in profusion all around. Strange white flowers which never seemed to open even in strong sunlight, brightly coloured hibiscus shrubs, and the rocks were covered in creepers where tiny birds hid and sang so sweetly for her as she relaxed.

The temptation to slip into the inviting water proved

too great for her on her second visit and became a habit. The spot was so deserted, not a single soul had appeared on any of her visits, that she felt quite safe to swim in her shift and then sit on the grass while her hair dried. In the warm air it took no time at all. She never mentioned the place to her father or anyone else. It was hers to enjoy. It was such a small thing to ask of life.

With the help of a sharp *adzes* she had purchased from the chandlery, she began to clear a plot of land behind the house. Simon had given her some melon seeds and half a dozen small orange trees. Perhaps they would survive and flourish, perhaps not, he had said, but she had accepted them, eager to become self-sufficient. She and her father could live well from their own home-grown vegetables and fruit. It would take time, but they were here to stay, she told herself doggedly as she toiled in the hot sun. How her back ached. The ground was so hard and unyielding, but she refused to be beaten. She did not know who, but someone had left a bag outside the door of the house which she had found early that morning. More seeds, but what they were she did not know. She had planted them regardless. Someone was obviously impressed by her determination and offering help, although too shy or perhaps too frightened to show it.

'Good lord, woman, are you out of your mind working in this heat?' a voice declared behind her in amazement.

The sun was in her eyes as she straightened, so that the features of the man on horseback were almost indistinguishable as she tried desperately to focus her gaze, but the voice was unmistakable! In an unconscious gesture of dismay her hand flew to her hair. Tiny wet ringlets smothered her forehead and cheeks. She pushed them back behind her ears, shutting out that memory of the day she had looked at herself in the mirror and seen a woman, not a child.

Ross pretended not to notice her distress as he swung himself from the saddle. What had brought him here? He had spent an enjoyable night with Lani, the morning with Tamori—as yet there was no word from the King but that did not surprise him, things worked very slowly in the islands—and he could have cut through a back trail to the house. Instead he had found himself heading for the village. Curiosity to see how they were faring? No. Simon had kept him up to date with everything. He wanted to see *her* again!

The sun was beginning to darken her skin in a most attractive way, but he knew he could not say so, not after what had happened between them. The way she looked at him told him she did not trust him. He had given her no reason to. Damnation! What was wrong with him. He did not want her, not in that sense, yet he was pleased to see her and know she was managing to cope with the rough existence thrust upon her.

'Captain Pendennis, good morning. If you are looking for my father he is not here.'

'I know. When I left the Prince's house, he was conversing with his three wives. He has been invited to stay for a meal so he will not be home for some while. I wondered if you would care to go riding?'

'I—I cannot. I have too much work to do.' Mary Kate's tone was far from friendly. He stepped towards her with a fierce frown as she swayed unsteadily and caught her fast by the wrist.

'You will be doing no more out here today unless you want to get sunstroke. Have you a hat? You should always wear one with your colouring.'

'You don't.' She looked at the blond hair, unprotected from the heat of the day. He did not look as if the excessive heat gave him a moment's trouble.

'I have been here far longer than you. Come inside and sit down. Have you something cool to drink? Some water?'

He gave her no chance to argue. Leading her inside, he seated her in one of the rocking chairs and looked around for a glass. What had been achieved in so short a time startled him. She had made curtains for the one window in the main room which Simon had inserted and matching covers for the cushions in the chairs. There were wild flowers in a painted jug on a table beneath it. He went into the room he could see had been chosen for the kitchen area. The stove was alight and the pot simmering on it gave forth an appetising smell. There were shelves on the walls to hold the crockery he had provided. Everything was as bright and clean as a new pin.

He found a glass and a pitcher of water, half-full. He filled the glass and took it back to her.

'Drink this and remain still for a while. Does your head ache?'

'No. My eyes do, just a little,' Mary Kate admitted reluctantly.

'If you don't have a hat, buy one tomorrow and wear it whenever you are out in the sun,' he warned, watching her through narrowed eyes. 'What were you doing out there anyway?'

'Planting seeds,' she returned indignantly. 'And the trees Simon gave me.'

'Do you know how to care for trees? Have you prepared the ground?'

She gave him a blank look and he sighed and perched himself on the edge of the table beside her.

'I'll send one of my boys down tomorrow with some

top soil. Let him do whatever is necessary. What else have you planted?'

'Melon seeds and . . . some I don't know. Someone left them outside for me to find.'

'Probably sweet potatoes, they will grow well enough. If you have any problems give me a call and I'll send someone down to take a look.'

'I should hate to inconvenience you, Captain. I am sure you are very busy,' Mary Kate said with iced sweetness. What was he doing here anyway?

'You haven't forgiven me, have you?' he asked, with quiet mockery, and her cheeks flamed.

'I'm sure I don't know what you mean.'

'Oh, yes you do. I kissed an attractive young woman and I see nothing wrong in that. You wanted it. I wanted it. It was pleasant. I did not mean to offend you. Haven't I given you long enough to forgive me? It has been three whole weeks.'

Was this his way of apologising, she wondered in amazement? The dark eyes were watching her with amusement, but he was not derisive as he had been so often before. She finished the drink and put the glass aside, feeling herself begin to grow cooler. What an idiot she was not to have considered the heat would affect her. She would do as he suggested first thing in the morning.

'There is nothing to forgive, Captain,' she said as she rose slowly to her feet. The stew was beginning to smell ready, she thought, and hurried into the kitchen to move it from the stove. If her father was eating with his royal host, he would not be very hungry when he returned. It would keep until tomorrow.

'Then you will come riding with me,' Ross said and she turned to face him in open-mouthed surprise. He had been serious?

'I—No. That is not possible.'

'You cannot do any more work outside today. I forbid it and your father will not be home until this evening. Why can't you spare a few hours to enjoy yourself?'

He made it sound so innocent—so inviting. Why not? No, she could not risk it. His very nearness made her feel as if she was being threatened by an unknown force. His eyes, his words challenged her and she wavered. Sensing it he urged,

'We can be back at the house in half an hour by the trail I will take. Mamalou can fix us a cold lunch. Simon and Kiki will be there if you feel the need for a chaperon. Wouldn't it be nice to see them again, you must have missed their company? Kiki has asked me to speak to you to try and make you come and live at the house where it is more comfortable. I told her you would not, but does that mean you will not meet her, let her know you do not regard her as an outcast? Your father's attitude has wounded her deeply.'

'I know. I didn't want that to happen. I like her and Simon is so in love with her.'

'After lunch,' Ross continued, seizing on her hesitation instead of an outright refusal to his offer, 'I could show you over the valley. I think you'd like to see what has been achieved there. Anything is possible if you get to know these people. Work with them instead of pushing them. They are not to be manipulated.'

'Are you suggesting my father would do such a thing?'

'In blind pursuit of what he believes in? Yes, I do,' he replied and she knew he was right.

'I have nothing suitable to wear for riding,' Mary Kate said lamely, recalling how her skirts had been pulled back over her knees before, for everyone to see her bare legs.

'My dear Miss Whitney,' Ross said, in a tone he might have used had he been addressing a small child. 'You are eight thousand miles from Boston. No one here who sees a pair of shapely legs is going to voice criticism or disapproval. You may not realise it yet, but you are among friends. What you do and how you act is entirely up to you. No one is going to sit in judgment of your actions.'

Except her father, Mary Kate thought and for a moment she almost refused his invitation. Then a smile lit up her features as she thought of the beautiful countryside she had seen around his house, the streams and lakes, the birds and trees. An hour or two. What harm was there in that? And he was being a perfect gentleman today, obviously regretting the way he had treated her.

'Very well, Captain. Give me a moment to make myself more presentable.'

They walked from the village to the house, through giant ferns where large butterflies sunned themselves in the heat of the afternoon. Beneath shady trees which offered moments of cool bliss away from the burning sun. Mary Kate had changed into a calico skirt and a blouse she had made from an old discarded dress. It was open at the neck and she had considerably shortened the long restricting sleeves which had fastened at the wrists before so that most of her arms were left bare. A touch of lace added to the plain collar had made all the difference, she had thought as she hastily tidied her hair before leaving. Perhaps Kiki had some material she did not want. Little by little she could make herself a whole new wardrobe, clothes more suitable for this new climate.

Ross spoke very little as they walked, but she did not

mind. This was the first time in three weeks she had had a chance to relax.

As soon as they neared the house, she noticed the instant change in both the land and the people. The latter were far more friendly, greeting them with waves or 'alohas' as they passed. The soil was rich, well-cultivated and well cared for. It would have taken many years to achieve and much hard work. Whatever her personal feelings for the man at her side, Mary Kate had to admit he had done well for himself and he was highly respected by everyone she spoke to.

Men working in a field off to her right caught her attention. They were moving slowly along row upon row of what looked for all the world to her like tall sword-shaped grasses.

'Pineapples. My latest venture I mentioned the other night,' Ross said, following her gaze and there was a note of pride in his voice.

'Pineapples,' she echoed. 'It looks like grass.'

'That will be three or four feet high before the actual fruit is ready to be harvested. It was a dream of my father's, but he died before we were able to cultivate the first area. I'm going to have them growing yonder towards the hills next year. I'll sell them to the ships in Honolulu harbour. From there they will probably go all over the world. One day,' he added with a smile. 'First, I have to grow this batch successfully. Maybe a prayer or two might help.'

'You are making fun of me. Why? Do you find it so hard to pray yourself, Captain, that you must mock others who can and who gain comfort from those prayers?'

'Comfort, or absolution for their sins? Forgive me, Lord, for I am a sinner, but I've told you so in a prayer, so please forgive me and I won't do it again. Until the next time,' he said, with mock gravity.

'I pity you your lack of faith.'

'Don't. I may not come up to your expectations of a good Christian, but I'm no hypocrite. I have my own set of rules for living and I abide by them. A different kind of faith, if you like. Faith in myself.' He paused to take a cigar from his pocket and light it, his black eyes narrowed against the glare of the sun as they looked at her. Damn it, he had not brought her out here to argue about faith. He just wanted to be with her. He would never know what had made him seek her company today, only that it had been necessary and he found it pleasant. If he kissed her now, he wondered, would she run from him as she had before? Or would the pretence of innocence disappear now that there was no one around to witness the intimacy he felt had risen unbidden between them?

He drew deeply on his cigar with a frown. He was mad to contemplate any kind of association with this girl. He had Lani and women of his choosing in any port he visited. What did he want with a strait-laced little puritan? He knew the devil in him wanted to break down that façade and expose the woman beneath, no different from any others he had known for a few short hours. Those wide blue eyes, as deep and mysterious as an inland lagoon, could look at him and he would think he was wrong. But he had felt the change in her that time he kissed her. The softness of her lips melting beneath his, the body which had been aroused by his hands. There was fire beneath the ice and the temptation to release it grew stronger as the days passed. She had pretended outrage that first time, yet she had come with him today.

'I think perhaps, in some ways, I have been wrong about you, Captain,' Mary Kate said quietly and it was those words which stopped his train of thought. 'You are good for these people. In your own way you are kind to them and you help them. I hope we will achieve the success you have.'

He could not deny the sincerity in her tone. He thrust what he had been contemplating to the back of his mind and looked down into her flushed face. He had not realised how small she was before, she barely came up to his shoulder. And so fragile. A strong gust of wind could blow her away. He suddenly wondered what it would be like to hear her say his name, instead of addressing him as Captain. So formal. So distant. Yet perhaps it was better things remained that way. She was getting beneath his skin in a way he did not like, did not want, did not understand. Better they remained at a distance lest he discover the ugliness which lay beneath the outward beauty.

And she was beautiful. Her skin had taken on a more healthy glow over the past weeks and those blue eyes shone like sapphires as she turned her gaze towards the house in the distance. She had liked his house, he knew that, wanted to stay, yet she had sided with her father in his decision to live in the village. Against her better judgment? Or because she was afraid of what he had aroused in her?

'You and your father are always welcome in my home,' he said and she looked up at him with a half-smile that told him she knew he was only being polite.

'You would both spend hours arguing and that would not be fair. Besides, he needs time to adjust . . . to finding Simon, I mean.'

He was sure she had not meant that at all.

'I hope to reunite us, you see,' she continued. 'It will take time, I know that. They are both so stubborn and

Simon is a man now. I cannot influence him, no more can Father. I want us all together, with Kiki. I like her so much and I am so happy for my brother. With her help and the King's approval, of course, I am sure we could do good here. Do not look at me like that, Captain. I mean what I say. I wish to start a school. From what I have seen of the wretched children, they would benefit from it.'

'If you take one child, then you will be given a dozen,' Ross told her in all seriousness. 'The parents will give you children to raise because they do not want them.'

'Then I will take them.' The answer came back without hesitation.

'Good God, woman, are you serious?' he ejaculated.

'Perfectly. If that is what they wish, I will care for their children.'

'And what of your own, Mary Kate.'

She blushed at the use of her name dropping so casually from his lips, and the thought she would be caring for the children of others and not her own.

'In time perhaps, I shall marry.'

'An uprighteous soul chosen by your father.'

'Why do you find it necessary to hurt me, Captain?' Mary Kate asked and his eyes narrowed to pin-points. She had touched that raw nerve again.

'You are easily hurt,' he replied bluntly and to his surprise she nodded.

'Yes, that is true, but I feel you take great delight in mocking me—humiliating me. Why? Is it only because I am a woman? Dear me, how she must have hurt your male pride that you want to subject all of us to the lash of your tongue.'

'She was a cheap whore who lied and cheated every day of her life.' Ross's voice was harsh with bitter memories, his eyes cold. 'She was my mother.'

'I'm sorry.' Mary Kate almost choked on the words. He would not want her pity. He was not that kind of man, but she had spoken before her mind had absorbed the shock of his words. 'I was very lucky, I had a wonderful mother. She would have loved your house. She gave up that way of living to marry Father and never regretted it.'

'Then she was a special kind of woman. One I don't believe exists,' Ross answered. 'Tell me about this paragon of virtue.'

He was deliberately trying to provoke her, Mary Kate realised, refusing to rise to the bait. His mother! And he hated her memory. That made her understand him a little better. That explained his determination to undermine her everyday existence, simple as it was. He did not believe because he could not. Faith in human nature, that closest to him as a mother should have been, had been destroyed. Perhaps if she told him of her own childhood, the love of giving, of sharing despite all the hardships, he would understand and in the end, forgive the poor unfortunate creature who was the object of his derision.

'My mother was the daughter of a titled Irish lord,' she told him, simply. She had never known that life, but her mother's memories she treasured. 'When Father asked for her hand, he was turned out of the house. He was only a poor Methodist preacher. Mother was a rich man's daughter, an heiress and a Catholic. She gave it all up to marry Father. She loved him that much.'

'She was a fool,' Ross declared in a hollow tone. The girl was a stupid romantic. 'She regretted it for the rest of her life no doubt.'

'No, she never did. At least, if there were regrets, I

never knew about them and we were very close. We have always been poor, but she never questioned what my father did. She loved him. She was with the man she loved. It was enough for her.'

'A virtuous woman? I don't believe it.'

'You have been unlucky, Captain. In all your women perhaps,' Mary Kate's voice held a sting of ice in it. 'There are some women who will sacrifice all to follow the man they love. You have not yet been fortunate enough to meet anyone like that.'

'I can do without a clinging vine, thank you,' Ross mocked but the remark did not make her bristle, as he had intended. Her eyes widened with amusement as she contemplated him.

'The Princess is a very independent spirit. You would not have that kind of trouble with her.'

The witch, he thought with begrudging admiration. She had sized Lani up after only a short while together. Clinging vine was what she was, although he would never admit it. Mary Kate Whitney had a mind of her own. He was pleased about that. She would give him back in rhetoric as good as he gave her. He liked that.

He took her arm with a friendly grin.

'I think you will do very well here, Mary Kate.'

'You are very forward, sir.' But she liked it!

'We are friends are we not?'

'Adversaries,' she countered. He was far too dangerous to be a friend.

'Now that I consider a challenge. You will lose, Mary Kate. Prepare yourself for that.'

Lose what? she wondered as he led her towards the house. She was in danger from only one thing and that was losing her heart to a man she knew would never care for her. Was she prepared for that?

CHAPTER
SIX

As IT happened, Ross and Mary Kate were not to spend the afternoon together. Simon was not at the house when they arrived, but there was a message from him to say that Hiponanu had arrived.

'One of Kamehameha's tax collectors,' Ross told her, with a grimace. 'I wonder what the old devil is going to try and sting me for this time? Damnation, why did he have to arrive today?'

'It doesn't matter,' Mary Kate said, hiding her disappointment. She had been looking forward to the ride around the plantation, to sharing a little of his domain, perhaps growing closer to him. 'Perhaps another time.'

'That's a promise. Make yourself comfortable while I find out where Simon has taken him,' Ross said and she sat down in a chair to await his return. He was away some ten minutes. Mamalou waddled into the room behind him, gave Mary Kate a warm greeting and began to lay the table for lunch.

'I really won't stay if you are going to be busy,' she said.

'Simon's taken him to see my grapevines up on the south ridge and probably sample last year's batch of wine. They won't be back for an hour at least. I am going to provide you with lunch. It's the least I can do. Afterwards I'll ride back to the village with you.'

'I'll walk. It's not far and I enjoy it. Besides, you will need to be here. Does everyone have to pay the King taxes?'

'Everyone. All land belongs to the King. He distributes some to people he likes or who have been loyal to him in times of trouble, to keep as long as he lives. They can do what they like with it so long as they remain obedient to his will and pay him taxes.'

'Do you mean if Kamehameha died this land would no longer belong to you?' Mary Kate asked incredulously. 'After all the work that has been done here? What a precarious way to live.'

'It would belong to the new King. In this case the heir apparent, Liholiho,' Ross answered with a nod. 'But I'm pretty much accepted around here as part of the scenery. I don't think I'd have any trouble. I know Liholiho. He'd make a lot of changes, but he's inclined to be more enlightened than his father and he'd like to see his people educated and given a better way of life than they have now, so people like you and your father would be welcomed on the islands if he was King. If anyone can influence Kamehameha into letting you stay, it will be him.'

'I think I like the sound of him,' Mary Kate said. It was nice to hear someone was on their side for a change. 'What will this Hiponanu take from you?'

'A bit of everything. He'll start off asking for half a dozen hogs, *awa*, hogsheads of my best rum, not to mention any other available liquor he can get his hands on. He'll want sacks of flour, sweet potatoes, vegetables and fruit.'

'All that?'

'He'll ask, I didn't say he would get,' Ross chuckled. 'We'll sit down and discuss it over a drink, or two or three. He has an insatiable thirst. By evening we should have agreed on a far smaller amount of everything and he'll go away well-fed, his thirst well-slaked and with only the things he was told to collect. It's a game, if you like. We play it every year. My father did before me. I've come to enjoy it. I know Hiponanu does. He's usually carried out of here.'

Mamalou provided them with large plates of pork, roast potatoes and fresh vegetables. Mary Kate's appetite was keen, but even so she could not manage everything.

'I know, I need to be fattened up,' she said laughingly when the woman stared at the plate,' but I truly cannot manage another mouthful. It was delicious, but far too much.'

Mamalou shook her head in obvious disapproval.

'You'll never find a man to look at you the way you are. Isn't that right, Ross?'

'From where I'm sitting, I think she looks fine,' Ross returned, his eyes slowly wandering over Mary Kate's trim figure and sunkissed cheeks which were beginning to deepen into a delightful shade of pink under his scrutiny.

'What are you thinking about?' Ross asked, as they sat on the verandah to drink their coffee. She had been lost in her own thoughts for some considerable time, unaware of his eyes on her. She had changed, he realised. A butterfly was emerging from the uninteresting chrysalis he had first known, still unaware of its potential in the world. When would she begin to try out those exciting new wings, he wondered? What would make her do so? 'Are you regretting coming here?' he asked.

'Here?' Mary Kate echoed and turned on him sapphire-blue eyes that held a hint of sadness in their depths. 'Where do you mean? Oahu? Or your home?'

'I'd like to hear what you have to say on both,' Ross returned candidly. The beauty he sensed radiating from her was different from anything he had ever known before. It was nothing that could be seen. He would not have called her beautiful. She did not have Lani's looks, or the attraction which drew him back time and time again to the woman who had been his mistress for over two years. It was as if there was something pure and bright deep within her that had just been released. Inner warmth that reached out and touched even his misogynist heart. Damnation, he thought, he was not about to get religion because of a moment's attraction. Or a single kiss.

'What was I thinking?' Mary Kate said quietly, her gaze returning to the stone outbuildings directly in her line of vision, where she knew beef was being salted and hung in readiness for not only the house and its inhabitants, but to be sold to the ships in Honolulu. It was one of his older ventures, Ross had told her. He had so many. He was a part of the island, a friend of the people. Although she wished it with all her heart and soul, she suspected that neither she nor her father would ever gain such respect, such acceptance. 'I have just begun to realise how much I want to belong. Don't look at me with that laughter in your eyes, I know you don't believe me. I don't think you even understand what I mean.'

'Enlighten me, then.' He lit a slim cigar and crossed long, booted legs, leaning back in his chair, his eyes almost closed as he waited for her to continue.

'Perhaps it would have been different if my mother had been alive to come with us. She had a way with her. It is in Simon. Something in him can reach people without him saying a word.'

Ross made no comment, although he knew exactly what she meant. The moment he had met Simon he liked him. The moment he and Kiki had been introduced, they had become friends. Lovers, within one short week, with his approval. Simon would never hurt his sister and they both knew it. The islanders had taken him to their hearts immediately. The way he sat with them for hours and listened to the wise ones, retelling tales of past warriors and victories over the enemies from distant islands. He was still young, yet he had blended into their way of life so easily. Like the sun which rose and set every day, taken for granted because it was always in the sky where it could be seen.

'She would have loved it here,' Mary Kate continued.

'More poverty. More heartbreak,' Ross intervened. 'Do you really believe she would have been happy?'

'Yes. By now she would have made so many friends. I—I don't even see the faces of whoever brings me milk and seeds, sometimes fruit, let alone know their names. I feel ashamed at that.'

'You must not. Tamori has made it plain that he does not want any of his people becoming involved with you until the King has sent him word.'

'So they feel sorry for the *haole* and his daughter in silence,' Mary Kate answered sadly. 'Not as sorry as I feel for myself, I assure you. I want to do so much.'

'If your father hopes to do anything, he will have to change his approach. And if he stays, tell him to watch Kalakui!'

'I will, but I dare not speak of it to him yet. Perhaps if we are allowed to stay, he will grow to realise the wisdom of a velvet glove. That is why I want Simon to come back to us. He can teach us all so much.'

'He will never set foot inside the house without Kiki.

You know that.' He could not find the words he suspected she was waiting to hear, that one day Simon would place his father above the woman he loved.

The sadness in her eyes deepened as she nodded. There was so much this man could tell her about Kiki to bring them closer, about the villagers so that she might understand them and their ways better, but he made no attempt to do so.

'Somehow I shall find a way. If all goes well, Captain, will you help me set up my school?'

Ross looked at her as if she had taken leave of her senses and, taking advantage of his surprise, she pressed home her point, adding,

'I have not yet thanked you for the roof we have over our heads, or the furniture you gave us. It was a truly Christian gesture. Were you so ashamed of being kind to people you do not like that you remained silent about it?'

'I was taught modesty is a virtue.' A smile touched Ross' mouth. 'I have very few virtues and I'm afraid I cannot boast that one as I would like to.'

'Then you are even more considerate than I thought. Will you give me men to work on the storeroom? I shall need tables and chairs too.'

'The children in these parts sit on the ground, Mary Kate, a dozen *tapa* mats would suit your purposes just as well,' came the dry retort, but he had not given an outright refusal to her plea for help and he saw hope rising in her face. 'Wait until you hear from Kamehameha. I'm not sticking my neck out any further for you until then.'

'And if we stay?' She would not let it rest. Her goal was almost in sight.

'Then you and I will have to discuss it in more detail.

Right now I have to get ready to receive Hiponanu. Are you sure you don't want me to ride back with you, or at least have one of the *kanakas* walk with you? I don't trust my life in the hands of the Almighty as you do. I know my enemies and I'm wary of them.'

'Are you saying there is anyone who would want to hurt us?' Mary Kate looked at him in surprise as she rose to her feet. She had not even considered that a possibility. Not wanted perhaps by everyone, but for someone to wish to inflict harm? Why? They had done nothing.

'Take my word for it, there are quite a few.' Ross gave an exasperated sigh. 'Ye gods, woman, what am I going to do with you? You'll have an escort whether you like it or not. His name is Hopi and he's the top boy here. You can trust him.'

She was beginning to trust Ross Pendennis, Mary Kate realised as she sat in one of the rocking chairs that afternoon and waited for her father to return. There was a certain charm about him she found fascinating. A dangerous charm which made her forget the kind of life he led, his total rejection of everything she held sacred, as she had done earlier when she had foolishly and boldly asked for his help. She had been expecting an outright refusal and was taken aback at the prospect of him actually providing more assistance. Why should he, unless it was in the hope of seeing her venture fail, proving to everyone how unsuitable the *haoles* were for the islands and their people. He would be able to say, look at this *haolewahine* who wishes to teach your children. Where is this God she tells you about that He does not come to her aid Himself? He expected failure. She would not contemplate it for one moment.

It grew dark and she lit the oil lamps and brought in more wood for the stove. Her father must be being entertained in fine style, and enjoying it, that he stayed away so long, she thought, as she settled down to continue with the making of new curtains. She considered it a good sign. She had put the stewpot back on the hob to reheat so that his supper would be ready for him if he wanted it.

There was more noise than usual coming from the other huts, she noticed. The sound of laughter and men singing. Another *luau* no doubt. The grog shop would be doing a brisk trade selling *awa* and spirits and in the morning there would be many thick heads. She was relieved her father was not at home to hear the uproar. On evenings like this, when there was a pleasant breeze and it was warm until well after dark, she would leave the door open so that she could watch the beautiful blood-red sunsets as she prepared dinner, or sit outside until her father looked at his watch and she knew it was time to retire. She knew the sounds of raucous revelry which often drifted to them made him want to leap to his feet and confront the offenders, Bible in hand. His face would darken and he would concentrate more fiercely on his reading, but she was aware of him listening to every sound, his imagination fired to envisage all manner of sinful activities being committed in the darkness.

Her eyes began to ache. As she put aside her sewing, she noticed the time. Ten o'clock. For the first time she began to feel slightly uneasy. The noise outside was not abating and she started nervously as someone rattled loudly on the paling with a stick. She was over reacting to what she had been told. She would not believe any of the villagers would harm them without reason.

She put the kettle on to make a pot of tea for herself as she always did before she went to bed and then remembered the stew. Lifting the lid she stared ruefully down at the dried vegetables and meat which now looked very unappetising.

She first noticed the glow outside the window as she came out of the bedroom after brushing her hair—a nightly ritual of thirty strokes which her mother had always insisted on. Mary Kate still continued with it even though she had seen her father's disapproving gaze on her. Somehow it brought her close again to the mother she had adored. Each day she grew more like her. The same eyes and hair. Was that the real reason he no longer liked her? Because she reminded him of the wife he had lost? The wife who had given up everything for love, only to find herself unwanted and worst of all, unloved?

As she sat in the chair, sipping her tea, she became aware that the glow she had thought to be torches outside was not only still there, but growing brighter, and there was an ominous flicker to the light that made her rise to her feet and move curiously towards the door. It looked almost like a fire.

She had seen one in Honolulu and it had remained vivid in her memory. The sight of the huts collapsing like matchsticks, each one bursting into flame like a tinderbox. Even with the help of seamen who had formed a bucket-chain to the water's edge, a dozen homes were lost. No one was hurt for everyone had simply run away, showing little or no concern for the loss of their homes and contents. Afterwards, she had been disgusted to learn, as soon as the fires had been extinguished, looters had gone from house to house systematically stripping them of anything worthwhile they could salvage from the ruins. A custom of the country, Duncan had told her with a shrug of his shoulders to indicate it happened every time there was a fire.

It *was* a fire, she realised in horror. She could see flames in the sky. Instead of singing, there were screams and shouting. She ran to the paling, flung open the gate and ran, as fast as her feet would carry her, towards the sounds.

The scene was chaotic. Already two houses were almost destroyed. Women and children were standing well back from the flames, making no attempt to try and contain them. No more were the men with them and Mary Kate saw, by the way they reeled and jostled one another, most of them were drunk. The only men attempting to do anything were from the *Moonflower*, who lived with women in the village, but the meagre amounts of water they could fling on to the fires were to little or no avail. Scorching hot cinders flew high into the night sky as one hut collapsed completely. Mary Kate heard an oath close at hand and someone grabbed her, pulling her back as some fell at her feet.

'Stay clear, miss.' It was Robert Langton, First Mate of the ship. His brother ran the grog shop. 'There's nothing we can do. I've some men clearing the ground on the other side, but it'll take a couple more huts at least before it hits that.'

'We can't just stand here and do nothing,' she protested angrily. 'Send some of those men to fetch water, lots of it, from the stream. We must dampen all the surrounding huts. The whole village could go up.'

'We've already done that with what little water we had here. We'll stop it from spreading, miss, don't worry, but that's all we must do. The house was cursed by the Kahuna Pule. We'd be torn to pieces if we tried to save it.'

'The what?' Mary Kate looked at him not understanding.

'Kalakui, the high priest. The husband and wife offended him and he cursed them and their children. That was yesterday. Tonight their house caught fire, proving his curse is powerful enough to destroy those who oppose him.' The man looked into her white face with sympathy. 'That's what you and your father are up against. Fear and taboos. It's what makes these people shun outsiders, reject anything new. I thought the Captain had tried to get that over to you already.'

'And the other huts that are going to be burned tonight?' she asked, watching the flames lick hungrily around the adjoining paling. A woman ran out, carrying a small child, dragging another behind her. 'That woman, is she cursed too?'

'We can't interfere. The flames are going in that direction, so she must have been given the "eye" by Kalakui too. It's as simple as that. It's the way these people believe.'

'It's horrible and so wrong,' Mary Kate cried. 'What's wrong? She's trying to go back and is being stopped. What is it?'

The woman was being forcibly restrained as she began to run back towards the hut. She fought and screamed at those who held her, dragging her slowly back in to the watching crowd, her eyes wide with terror.

'Her youngest child is still in there. She couldn't carry all three . . . Miss Whitney, don't be a fool! Come back here . . .'

Mary Kate struck aside the hand which fastened on her arm. A grim-faced *kanaka* stepped out in front of her as she headed determinedly towards the doomed hut. Cinders which had landed on the roof had set alight the straw and smoke was pouring out through the doorway.

'Stand aside.' She glared at him, daring him to try and

restrain her. He caught her by the wrist and she struck him full in the face, hardly caring what she had to do to make him release her. They might be able to stand there and watch while an innocent child was sacrificed to the whim of their high priest. She could not. Even at the cost of her own life, although it was not until afterwards she realised how reckless and uncaring of her own life she had been.

The man raised a clenched fist before her wide eyes. He was going to knock her down! And then, she never knew what happened to make him change his mind, but as she threw back her head to stare up into his eyes, she was aware of something near to astonishment creeping over his face. He jumped back from her as if touched by one of the red-hot flames which were now so close, everything around them looked as if it was bathed in blood. Everything—and everyone. Ross explained later and she understood.

At that moment, however, all she knew was that her way was clear. She heard a chorus of voices behind her as she ran into the swirling smoke, and over them the roar of flames above her as the fire consumed the roof. She did not see the child, she fell over it, unable to see anything at all in those blinding, terrible moments, as she sprawled in the dust beside the limp form of a little boy of about three.

The heat was unbearable. Fragments of straw, burning fiercely, fell on her as she tried to regain her feet with the child in her arms. She cried out in pain as they seared her bare arms, struggled to brush them off without losing her hold on the unconscious youngster. She could not see the door, only fire. She was going to be burned alive. Dear God, no! She could not die, not yet—she had so much to do. Had she been brought to these ignorant, frightened people, to die without achieving anything?

She fell on her knees, choking with the smoke, eyes streaming, her outstretched hand groping for the wall, wincing in pain as splinters of bamboo cut into it. Shuffling forward an inch at a time, dreading a sudden sound above her head which would tell her the roof was about to collapse and bury them both. The wall came to an end and she fell, rather than crawled out into the open. The tears which came then were of relief, rather than fear—and of joy. She did not feel the pain in her arms or hands as she staggered to her feet and through red, streaming eyes held out the child to the mother. The woman did not move. Not only she, but all the villagers were staring at her in awe. Like shadows they began to melt away into the darkness behind them until only the mother was left. The last of Mary Kate's self-control snapped.

'What's the matter with you? Take your child. He's not dead, he's alive. Take him. Look after him,' she cried in exasperation. 'What's wrong with you, did you want him to die in there?'

'Give him to me, miss.' Robert Langton gently relieved her of her burden. She stood swaying unsteadily as he handed the boy to its mother. What he said to her, Mary Kate did not understand, but it brought the woman out of her trance-like state.

Clutching the boy to her breast she came to Mary Kate, went down on her knees and solemnly kissed the hem of her skirt, still smouldering in places from the red-hot cinders, and touched her forehead to the ground.

'Get up. Oh, please don't do that. You mustn't. Tell her she must not, Mr Langton.'

'It is the homage due to one of the "chosen ones of Pele",' the man returned quietly. He pulled the woman to her feet and firmly pushed her back. 'You'll be getting a lot of that from them now. By God, miss, that was the bravest thing I've seen in a long time. Let me help you home. I'll send someone in all haste for your brother, you'll need those burns seeing to. And look at your hair. No wonder you put the fear of Christ, beggin' your pardon, miss, into the *kanakas*.'

'I—I don't understand,' Mary Kate murmured weakly. She was beginning to feel the pain now, in her arms and hands and her cheeks felt as if they were on fire themselves. What was wrong with her hair? Her searching fingers found the loose tresses had been singed in places. When she drew her hand away, she saw it was covered in blood from the splintered bamboo. Without a sound she folded on to the ground like a rag doll at the First Mate's feet.

'Lie still,' Simon insisted for the third time as Mary Kate tried to raise herself from the bed. 'I'm the doctor and you'll damned well do as I tell you.'

'Don't swear,' she said, but her voice held no reprimand this time and she fell back on to the pillow with a grimace of pain. 'Is my hair very badly burned?'

'Don't let Father hear you ask me that again or he'll be lecturing you on the sin of vanity. No, it isn't, nor are the burns on your arms serious, but these hands will have to stay bandaged for several days. I'll come back tomorrow and see them again. Until I do, you will rest. That's an order.'

Simon moved back from her, his eyes still slightly dazed from what he had found when he rushed into the hut, brought by a message that his sister had been badly burned in a fire. Mary Kate had been lying unconscious on the bed, her clothes torn and blackened from the smoke, as was her face. The tangled red hair was spread out over the pillow like tongues of the fire he had passed as he spurred his horse headlong through the village with Ross not a yard behind him. They had been in the middle of an evening meal with Tamori and Hiponanu when the garbled message which arrived sent them racing to their horses in a state of near panic.

'Yes, Doctor,' Mary Kate answered meekly, with no intention of obeying him. After a good night's rest she would feel fine again.

'My sister, the heroine,' her brother said quietly, his hand covering hers. 'I'm very proud of you. It was a brave thing you did.'

'And a very foolish one,' Ross remarked from the doorway. 'Langton tells me the roof collapsed seconds after you got out. You could have been killed.'

'I—I didn't stop to think about that,' Mary Kate said, defensively. 'The child was inside . . .' He sounded almost concerned.

'Apart from risking your own life you have also invited Kalakui's anger. He's not a man to be trifled with, Mary Kate. He won't forget you have broken his taboo.'

'You too! You would have let him burn in there? I don't believe that. You couldn't have stood there and watched like they did.'

He advanced to the bed and stared down at her, a half-smile on his face. He would have done exactly the same as her and he knew it!

'Perhaps not. Anyway, as it happens, it has turned out for the best. The boy is safe and you, I think, will find tomorrow everyone has now accepted the "chosen one of Pele". You must have made quite an exit. I'd like to have seen it.'

'What are you talking about?' Simon asked, with a frown.

'Mr Langton called me that too,' Mary Kate said. 'What have I to do with their fire goddess?'

'They think you are one of her ambassadors on earth. It happens sometimes, usually with Kalakui choosing the person he would like to have a little more power in the village. He will decide a man or woman has been chosen by one of the gods to take on human form. It's a great way of controlling the masses and it works very well. Make the most of it while you can.' Ross thrust his hands deep into his pockets. 'That red hair must have given them the fright of their lives. Langton said you came out of the hut surrounded by flames. It was as if you were on fire yourself, everything was so red.'

'But they've all seen my red hair before,' Mary Kate protested. A goddess! How she could use that if she wanted to, but she would not. It would be too cruel to take advantage of these simple-minded people.

'Not like it is now,' he went on. 'Look at it. Loose like that it has fire in it. Like Pele's. They must have thought they were looking at Pele herself for a moment. Take my advice and press home with the advantage offered. It will put Kalukui's back up, but I'll keep an eye on him.'

'No, it would not be right—or fair.'

'Damnation! What has being fair to do with it?' Ross ejaculated. 'You will be accepted now. That's all that matters to you, isn't it?'

'Because they think I am chosen by Pele?'

'Ross is right. What you have done tonight has tipped the scales in your favour,' Simon agreed. 'You risked your life and saved a child from certain death. To accept the friendship they will offer is small thanks, but more than you have been getting up to now.'

'I don't know.' Mary Kate raised a hand to her forehead which had begun to throb maddeningly. 'I—I can't think now. I'll have to speak with Father . . . Simon, where is he? Have you seen him? He's been away all day.'

'He left Tamori when we arrived,' Ross replied. 'He said he was going to walk for a while.'

'I think he rather wanted to be alone. The good news overwhelmed him. I've never seen him so excited,' Simon said, and he smiled down into her anxious features. 'He'll be back later, don't worry. He's probably alone with God somewhere, thanking the Almighty for his good fortune.'

'You really can be most irreverent at times,' his sister chided, 'and annoying. What news?'

'The King has sent word to Tamori through Hiponanu that you may stay so long as you cause no trouble among the villagers. You may build your school, Mary Kate. I'll even provide the *tapa* mats,' Ross added with cool mockery. 'Just to prove I can be as good a Christian as the next man.'

'Good heavens, you'll be getting him to Sunday services next,' Simon chuckled. He liked this friendship which seemed to be developing between the two of them and he intended to encourage it in every way.

'That I draw the line at. I'm going back to the house now. Are you coming?'

'No, I'll stay until Father returns. I don't want to leave Mary Kate alone.'

'I'll say goodnight then.' Ross bent over the bed and brushed a kiss as light as a breath of wind across her mouth. 'Sleep well, Firehair.'

'Well I'm damned,' Simon murmured after his departing figure.

Mary Kate pretended not to hear him. She could not
have been more thunderstruck if a bolt of lightning
had burst into the room. Now she understood the love
which had tied her mother to a man who did not care for
her. If he had asked it of her at that moment, she
would have followed Ross Pendennis into the fires of
hell.

Mary Kate was working in the *pauku*, which she had
learned was the name for her small vegetable patch
when Kiki arrived with Simon. Another bag of seeds had
been outside the door when she opened it and she had
spent the past hour planting them, feeling unseen eyes
on her as she did so.

'Did you ever intend obeying my instructions?' Simon
asked sternly as he lowered Kiki to the ground and
climbed down after her. 'Look at those bandages!
Covered in dirt. Come inside and I'll redress those
hands.'

'Yes, Doctor,' Mary Kate answered meekly, a smile
on her lips as she passed him. 'Hello, Kiki. Will you
come inside while I make some tea?'

'No, thank you.' The girl remained hesitantly by the
door. She wanted to follow them, Mary Kate knew, but
she was afraid of the man who preached Christianity, yet
could not find it in his heart to accept the woman his son
had chosen to love. She was better able to understand,
now that she too was in love, how it changed one's
outlook on life, in a very short time. Was it her imagination, or did the birds sing sweeter this morning? The
sky look bluer? The warmth of the sun on her face made
her want to walk and enjoy it, not stay inside the house,

shutting out these things that were, this morning, so much more inviting to her.

'Where is he?' Simon asked as he too, paused on the threshold.

'Next door, inspecting the storeroom. We are going to start work on it as soon as we can get some help.' His sister's face lit up with enthusiasm.

'You will do no such thing. Those hands need time to heal,' her brother returned with a frown. 'Anyway, Ross can't spare any workers for a few days. We're sailing for the Big Island tonight with Hiponanu. He thought it might be a good idea, as he has to return the tax collector home safely anyway, to see the King and convey personally your gratitude for being allowed to stay. Kamehameha will appreciate that. There is something you should know. Ross has given Tamori his personal assurance that his people will not be forced into anything. He said something about a velvet glove! If anything goes wrong you realise the responsibility will fall on his shoulders. Kalakui has been waiting for just such an opportunity for years. If he could oust Ross from the Prince's side, turn them into enemies . . .'

'That will not happen, I promise you,' Mary Kate said quietly. 'Thank Captain Pendennis for me. I appreciate all that he has done and is doing.'

'The two of you seem to be getting on well,' Simon remarked as he gently replaced the soiled bandages with fresh ones. 'He's not such a blackguard as you thought, is he?'

'He is arrogant—proud—wilful—conceited . . . but no,' she confessed, 'not quite as bad as I thought. He has been very kind to us.'

'He'll arrange for some *kanakas* to come down and start work as soon as we get back. There's some *tapa* mats to come and he thinks he might be able to find a few tables. Nothing remarkable, just practical.'

'That's wonderful,' Mary Kate exclaimed. 'It's a start, Simon.'

'Now all you have to do is persuade the parents to bring their children here to be taught the ways of the *haoles*.'

'No. I don't want to change their way of life, only their ignorant beliefs,' she insisted. 'They are like easily led children, Simon.'

'And the new teacher intends to take a firm hand with them.'

'You sound like your captain. That's the kind of remark I would expect from him. He doesn't think I'll succeed either. Maybe that's why he's being so helpful.'

'You do the man a great injustice, Mary Kate. He may not be your idea of the perfect human being, but his heart is in the right place. He's stuck his neck out for you too when he didn't have to. He stands between you and Kalakui and believe me, that's no mean feat. He's given you the chance you wanted. Take it, but for God's sake, don't abuse it or you will lose everything. There, that's more presentable. I have to leave now. I'll look in when I get back.'

'Does Kiki have to go back with you?' Mary Kate asked as they returned outside. 'I have some shopping to do and it would be nice to have some company.'

'That's up to her.' Simon looked enquiringly at the girl who nodded, with a shy smile. He took her in his arms and kissed her soundly on the lips. 'I'll see you when I get back. Are you really sure?'

'I would like to show the "chosen one of Pele" her sacred pool,' Kiki said.

'Do you think that wise?'

'It is her place, is it not? Why should she not go there?'

'I could give you a dozen reasons, but I can see you've got your mind set on this. Very well, go ahead.'

'Won't you see Father before you go?' Mary Kate pleaded, but her brother shook his head.

'He saw me ride up. He knows I'm here. He won't come out and I won't go in. You should accept there will never be a reconciliation between us.'

'No, I won't.' She kissed him on both cheeks and watched him ride away, saddened by his words. But then as she turned and found Kiki waiting patiently for her, she brightened again and took the girl by the hand. 'Come and help me do some shopping and then we will find this special place of Pele's.'

CHAPTER
SEVEN

'THERE.' Kiki pointed along the path ahead of them. 'Pele's sacred place is beyond those trees. It is not allowed for me to come further with you. Only when the high priest Kalakui is present is anyone allowed there.'

Mary Kate knew what lay ahead of her. Without knowing it, the girl had brought her to the place she had discovered on her first walk and the pool which had become her own particular little piece of paradise.

'I have been here before,' she confessed, 'But I did not know it was a sacred place. Your gods are not mine, Kiki, but I would not want to cause trouble with Kalakui. I know he does not like either Father or myself for the new ways we have brought with us.'

'The "chosen one of Pele" may go where she pleases.'

Kiki did not show the least surprise at the announcement. It was almost as if she knew of those secretive excursions away from the house, but how could she? Mary Kate had always been so careful to ensure she was not seen. No one suspected she came here to swim and be alone with her thoughts, amid the sweet-smelling night flowers and the sound of the wind in the *kukui* trees. She dismissed the thought as pure imagination and started along the path, then realising the girl was not following, turned back and beckoned. 'Come. There is nothing here to hurt you.'

'No. It is *kapu*. Forbidden.'

'And do you think Kalakui would dare argue with me, whom Pele has favoured?' Mary Kate asked boldly. 'I want you to accompany me, Kiki.'

Without a word the girl followed her to the pool and they sat down together at the water's edge.

'Do you really believe in the old ways?' Mary Kate continued. 'Surely Simon or Captain Pendennis have not left you in total ignorance? Your English is perfect. Who taught you that?'

'Ross, my brother. My mother has taught me what you call the old ways. She no longer believes in them as she used to and Ross protects her from Kalakui's reprisals because of his friendship with Tamori, but it is not always easy for him. They are deadly enemies. Because of the Princess too. Kalakui would rule us in the Prince's place with her as his consort. He has much power. Many are afraid of him. Afraid of his great magic.'

'That is the first illusion we must dispense with. He is no magician. He has no power, but he probably has many people so afraid of him they will do anything to please him. Like setting fire to those houses last night. I could not believe my eyes. People standing around like statues, watching them burn, that little boy.' Mary Kate shuddered at the recollection and Kiki's liquid brown eyes were suddenly sympathetic.

'When my brother came home last night and told us what you had done, my mother was afraid for you, but he told her he would protect you and your father. I found that strange. He does not like people very often. Do you understand me? He is a kind man, but . . . how do you say . . . distant? Even my mother and I know there is a small part of him that is lost even to us. A part of him he will not let anyone see.'

The part which contains all the hate and contempt he

held for his mother and after her, all women, Mary Kate thought sadly. She loved a man incapable of loving, of giving himself totally to anyone. If only she had the strength of will to fight for his soul, but she had not. She did not want to lead the kind of life her mother had done. Unwanted, unloved and unrewarded by the man to whom she devoted every moment of her time, every breath in her body. If she thought for one moment Ross might ever look at her with love in his eyes . . . It was like wishing for the moon and she was much too level-headed a person to do that.

'We are a burden he does not want, I know that.'

'You would be better for him than the Princess. She is as evil as Kalakui. Together they would destroy her own brother and then, I think, she would destroy him. In time perhaps Ross . . .'

'I doubt that. Your brother is far too sure of himself for that. As you say, he does not share all of himself with anyone. Unless he does, no one can ever hurt him.'

'You are very wise,' Kiki said solemnly and Mary Kate laughed. 'Perhaps after all, you are someone special. If you are not, how did you come to this place and it pleased you, when you did not know what it meant? Did Pele not bring you here?'

'No, she did not. Any more than she endowed me with red hair when I was born.'

'Some mysteries cannot be explained.' Kiki's smile was almost mischievous. 'I heard it said in the village this morning that you are the figurehead on the *Moonflower* come to life, to protect the man you love because he has chosen to remain on the land for so long instead of returning to the sea.'

'What nonsense,' Mary Kate declared. Her thoughts

flew back to that day at Ross' house, and that room that
was so very special to him and the brazen, half-naked
figurehead on the painting which Tamori had had carved
as a present for the new ship. 'I hope my father does not
hear such gossip. He would be furious.'

'He has come only to change, Simon said. You will
listen. You are wise, like my brother. The island has
accepted you. I feel it here.' The girl touched her heart.
'My people look upon you with respect now. That is
good. You will be able to grow close to them, but you
will also learn their ways. I wonder who will change
who?'

Why should those words fill her with such
apprehension, Mary Kate wondered? She had accepted
her new life and she loved her new home. In time she
would make the house more comfortable than the one in
Boston. The school she longed for was no longer just a
dream. Why then, should she fear a change in herself?
The opportunity was before her, yet she was afraid to
reach out and grasp it. It was wrong, she told herself, to
take advantage of people who knew no better. She felt
confused and more than a little afraid of this new role
that had been thrust upon her. Accept it, Simon had told
her. Use it, had been the advice of Ross Rendennis, but
she did not have his singularity of mind. She was not
capable of using people as he was. To him, it was second
nature.

'Why is this place so special to Pele?' She thought it
time to change the topic of conversation.

'A long time ago, when the Big Mountain was alive,'
Kiki said, pointing above their heads to the enormous
volcano which dominated the scene, 'Pele would warn
my people of her displeasure by turning the waters of
this pool as red as the fire she sent down from the

mountain to destroy all in its path. It has not happened for many, many years, but Kalakui still prophesies the fire water will come again and the river of destruction will cover everything, houses and people, if we stray from the old ways.'

An extinct volcano, Mary Kate realised and a man who traded on the fears of others to keep them subject to his domination. She was ashamed of the comparison which came immediately to her mind. Kalakui and her father!

She trailed her fingers in the water. It was cool, inviting, spurring her on to recklessness.

'Shall we take advantage of Pele's generosity? Let us swim.'

'I dare not.' The girl was quite taken aback by the suggestion, for all her knowledge of the outside world which Ross and Simon must have given her. Here it was different. Here there was Kalakui. 'If I am found here . . .'

'Then why did you bring me here?' Mary Kate asked quietly. 'Trust me, Kiki. Are we not friends? I will allow no one to hurt you.'

Kiki's eyes widened as she began to unfasten her blouse, then removed it and took off her shoes and stockings. Last of all her skirt. As she took the combs and pins from her hair, she was aware of the girl's expression changing, as that of the *kanaka* had done when she had challenged him the night before. Kiki was struggling to decide which she wanted to accept, which world she wanted to belong to. It was not going to be an easy decision. Without further hesitation Mary Kate turned and dived into the water. As she surfaced, she saw the girl beside her and her face broke into a smile. They were becoming friends despite all the obstacles in their path. At that moment she could not have been happier.

When they returned to the village an hour later, Mary Kate having carefully arranged her hair back into its matronly knot before she approached the house, she saw the mother of the boy she had saved, hovering before the paling. She was carrying a basket of fish. Kiki spoke to her for a moment, took it from her and handed it to her companion.

'Her husband went out this morning to get these for you, as thanks for what you did. They are poor people, they do not have much to offer, except their thanks. If you wish, he will do this every morning for you.'

'Oh, no. It is very kind, but no. Tell her, I am grateful for her kindness. A few fish sometimes would be most welcome, but he must think first of her and his family. We have all we need.'

'Like them you have very little,' Kiki said, giving her a strange look. 'But you share so much of yourself. Do you love people so much?'

'I believe it is better to give, than to receive. It is the Christian way. It is a good way to live.'

'It is our way. We are not so different after all. What does this God of yours ask in return for his protection?'

'Devotion. Loyalty and love.'

'Not the lives of those who offend him?'

'Never. It is wrong to take the life of another human being, Kiki. Has no one ever told you that?' She was appalled that Simon had never talked to her of right and wrong.

'Ross calls Kalakui a bloody butcher. He has said it many times.'

Mary Kate felt the colour rise to her cheeks at the girl's casual use of such words. She would never have expressed herself so, but she agreed with him.

'A very colourful way of expressing himself when he is no doubt angry.'

'Oh, no. He says he would like to strangle him. You have never seen my brother in a rage. He is like the Big Mountain in full fury. One day he will kill Kalakui. It is the only way of saving his own life,' Kiki returned calmly. 'I must go now. Will you come to the house soon? My mother and I would like it very much.'

'As soon as I can,' Mary Kate promised. 'Please thank the woman for me.'

'Her name is Nuina. If you wish, until your hands are better she will come and clean for you and cook your meals.'

It was a sensible idea, Mary Kate thought, looking down at her bandaged hands. The water had helped to ease the throbbing, but she would be quite useless at preparing a meal for several days. Her father could not object to such a kind offer to help.

'Tell her I shall be most grateful for her help. I will take the fish to my father and tell him she will be helping us for a few days.'

Mary Kate found her father busily hammering nails into the paling at the back of the storeroom, sealing off a back entrance. Sweat glistened on his brow from his labours and she saw his hands were covered with dirt. She had never seen him so enthusiastic over a project as to launch into the work himself. He had always stood on the sidelines, giving instructions, but never joining in. She felt a momentary pang of regret that they were not working together.

'Father, look! The woman whose son I saved last night has brought us these fish. Isn't that kind? And she has offered to stay and cook for us and help around the house until my hands are better. I have accepted her kind offer. I felt sure you would not mind.'

Nathaniel paused and turned to look at her. For a terrible moment she thought he would refuse to offer, then he smiled. At least the nearest thing to a smile she had seen since they had left Boston. It made her feel quite elated. Was he beginning to feel a part of the island too, as she was? Willing to work for its good and the benefit of its people, not dictate to them and expect them to accept his own beliefs without a murmur? How wonderful it would be were it so.

'The Lord moves in mysterious ways, Mary Kate.' He rarely called her anything but 'my daughter' these days. 'You have been favoured in His eyes, do you realise that? I knew one day it must happen.'

'You—you don't mind this nonsense about me being one of Pele's chosen ones?'

'Nonsense? It is His will, don't you realise that? He has shown me the way at last. I was lost and He has found me. Found us all and brought us together so strong, nothing and no one can ever break us apart again. He has shown us the way to their hearts and we will use it.'

In his way he was proud of what she had done, but she knew he would never admit it. *God* had made her rush into the blazing hut and snatch the child from certain death. *He* had placed the comparison between her likeness and that of Pele into the minds of the villagers!

Perhaps he had, Mary Kate thought, but remembering the roar of the flames and the intense heat that had threatened her, she found it hard to accept she had not been in danger.

'Are you doubting His wisdom?' Nathaniel asked, staring at her from beneath furrowed brows. 'My child, listen to me. He guided our footsteps here, to Simon. To reunite us and now we are together, we must stand firm and strong in the face of the opposition. The Prince is with us, I have his assurance on that. You may open your school and on Sundays we will hold services. You and Simon and I. My prayers have become reality. When I am gone, your brother will stand by your side and continue my work. That is how it was meant to be.'

'No, Father,' Mary Kate cried, suddenly realising his trend of thinking. 'Simon is not with us. You know that. What we have to achieve can be done without him. It has to be, he has another life now with his wife. You must accept that.'

'What!' Her father's eyes blazed. 'You expect me to accept what is not the Lord's will. He brought us here, I tell you! We are but instruments of His will. We will do what has to be done, all three of us. Without that woman Simon will return to us, you'll see. In time, he will abandon all that which he knows is sinful. He will be shown the way as I was.'

'I will not let you hurt them,' Mary Kate whispered, her eyes brimming with sudden tears. The brief moments of happiness she had shared with Kiki that morning were destroyed in an instant by the words thrown at her. 'They are in love, Father. Must you destroy them because you have never known it?'

She turned and ran from him, from the anger on his face and the sudden fear in her heart, because she now knew all her earlier suspicions had been right. And one more frightening thing had become apparent. Her father wanted to bring Simon back into the fold, separate him from the woman he loved. How, she did not know, but to succeed it would have to be something so drastic it destroyed one of them.

Kiki stood outside the storeroom, her face white with

pain, and instantly Mary Kate knew she had overheard the whole of the conversation.

'I'm sorry.' She took the girl in her arms and held her, knowing it was of little comfort to either of them. 'I pray every night he will change, but now he uses this likeness to Pele to his advantage and it frightens me, Kiki. It is not the way.'

'Perhaps if he held new life in his hands, his grand-child,' the girl whispered brokenly. 'Would that help him?'

'You—you are with child?' Mary Kate breathed. 'Kiki, that's wonderful.'

For Simon and Kiki and Ross and Mamalou, but not her father! A child born out of wedlock. He would never accept it!

'I see by your face it pleases only you,' Kiki said with a shrug of her shoulders. 'Simon said that was how it would be. Is it so important to your father that I am wife to his son by his laws? I have cooked for him and kept his house. I have nursed him when he was sick and I have been true to him. I had not known a man before him. I have taken no other since the *tapa* covered us. What else must I do? Why must I do anything else? Ross has no harsh words for me, no more do you. Only him. Why do I feel it necessary to please a man who will not look into my eyes?'

'Kiki, don't torture yourself,' Mary Kate begged. 'I can't tell you the child will change everything, because I don't think it will, but if it makes you and Simon happy, then that is all that matters. Think of no one else but the man you love, as you have always done.'

Kiki laid a hand against Mary Kate's breast, a look of pain in her eyes.

'I feel doubt in you. Regret. I bring pain to you.'

'No. Never think that. I love my brother and I have come to love you, Kiki. Never doubt that.'

'But because of me you and your father argue. You ran out in tears. I must not—I will not come between you. Perhaps my husband has not been wise in his words to me. He has no love for the man whose blood is in him. I must think on this more. As you are an instrument, was that not what he called it, of your God, perhaps I am one of mine. To be used to bring us all together. That would be good, would it not?'

'Kiki, I don't understand. Please, do nothing to harm what you have with Simon.' The words had begun to make Mary Kate feel uneasy. What strange notion had her father's outburst put into the girl's head? 'The love you share is the most important thing you both have. Let nothing come between you.'

Kiki withdrew from her embrace, a strange smile on her pretty features.

'I have told Nuina you are pleased with her offer. She will stay with you and do whatever you wish. *Aloha*, we will see each other again soon.'

'Why are you wearing your hair like that?'

Nathaniel looked across at Mary Kate as she sat reading one evening, his gaze fastened on the loose curls about her shoulders. He had ignored them the first day, but now they annoyed him. They made her look too much like her mother, made him remember the past when she had been young and pretty and he had still had hopes for his future.

'It is difficult to do anything with it with my hands bandaged,' she returned quietly. 'Do you not approve? It feels so pleasant for a change. It's nice not to look into the mirror and find an old maid staring back at me.'

By the sudden hardening of his face she knew she had chosen the wrong words. For several minutes he continued to stare out through the window, but again she felt his eyes return to her and knew there was more condemnation to come. Since the day she had spoken out against him in defence of Kiki, she had sensed his displeasure. She had stayed out of his way during the day, teaching Nuina how to sew, when she had finished the household chores, or walking with her to the river to fetch fresh water. At night little conversation passed between them if it did not concern the new schoolroom.

Three days after Kiki's visit, workmen arrived from Ross' plantation, bringing with them mats and tables. They set to on the storeroom with a fervour that needed no encouragement from the man who watched them every moment of the day. Another week and she could begin her first class, Mary Kate had thought that very morning and now her father sat a few feet away from her and she felt, once again, that small happiness slipping away from her.

'You are too much like your mother,' Nathaniel said, closing the Bible on his lap. 'She, too, spent too much time admiring herself when she should have been engaged in better occupations.'

'That is not fair.' His daughter rose immediately to the defence of the mother she had always considered no less than perfect. 'She never gave you any cause for complaint, even though you were . . .' This time the flint grey eyes which registered their warning, did not daunt her. 'Even though you were at times the most unfeeling man I have ever seen. No word of thanks ever passed your lips for all her labours. There were times I heard her cry herself to sleep because she felt so alone. It was cruel of you to treat her as you did.'

'That is enough! You have no idea what you are saying.'

'I have and I must say it. There must be truth between us if we are to continue with our work here. It cannot be achieved at the cost of others, don't you understand that?'

Mary Kate's eyes sparked defiance such as he had never seen before. No, that was not true! Once before, when Maureen had stood before her father and declared her love for him, her determination to marry him whatever the cost! It was like looking at a ghost! All those years of self-pity, of humiliation and poverty rose up to taunt him and as he had no wife now to vent his anger on, it was directed at his daughter—her daughter, who chose to defy him. To remind him of the hypocrite he really was!

'Why should Mother not have been proud of the gifts with which God endowed her? She was beautiful. Why did you never tell her so? It is not a sin.'

'And who has told you so?' Nathaniel rose from his chair, his voice like granite. 'I have seen you staring into the mirror of late. Ever since we came back from the Captain's house, if I remember rightly. I also remember your eyes were red when you came down to dinner. You had been crying. Did he think you pretty? What did you see when you looked into his eyes? Tell me? Did you see the lust in your own soul as I see it when I look at you now? God has smiled on you and you have chosen to use His favour for your own ends. Did he reject you? What have you to offer him when he has his Princess? If I am any judge of character he found you amusing. He played with you as he has doubtless done with scores of loose women on every trip he makes. An hour's pleasure—if that—and then you are forgotten.'

'You—you are comparing me to—women like that?' Mary Kate stammered. She knew her cheeks had flooded with bright colour for his words had brought vividly to mind that encounter at the house when Ross had first kissed her. He made it sound dirty! Made her feel unclean!

'Did he kiss you?' her father demanded. 'Yes, I can see by your face he did and you enjoyed it. You and Simon both, have much to learn. In time you will learn to control the passions of the flesh, as I did. Hard work is what you both need. Hard work and constant prayer.'

'To turn me into an old woman before my time like my mother and Simon into another you?' Mary Kate cried.

'You have said enough. Go to your room.'

Mary Kate went into her bedroom and came out again a moment later, a shawl about her shoulders. Head thrown back, she faced her father undaunted.

'I will not be treated as a child any longer, Father. I am going for a walk.'

'To meet him?' Nathaniel accused. His hands had clenched into tight fists at his sides and there was a moment when she thought he might strike her for such open defiance of his authority. 'Go to him then, but do not come back here. He will discard you soon enough and then you will be glad I am here to receive you.'

'No, I am not going to meet him or anyone else,' Mary Kate said through tight lips. 'I shall be no longer than an hour. I—we have both spoken hastily. We should be alone for a while, don't you think?'

Nathaniel turned his back on her, returned to his chair and began reading again. She walked slowly away from the house, when she wanted to run, but knowing he was watching her through the window, she kept a steady pace, hugging the shawl tightly about her shoulders. She had not penetrated his defensive shield one iota and had only succeeded in widening the gulf between them. What was she to do? It was becoming impossible to live beneath the same roof together without angry words passing between them at least once a week.

Had he guessed her secret, she wondered and decided he had not. He thought she had been engaged in a mild flirtation with Ross and had been rejected. She dreaded to think of the name he would have used for her had he known she had fallen in love with the man who was the embodiment of everything he sought to destroy on the island.

The weather had changed that afternoon and dark storm clouds heralded the approach of rain. She would walk as far as the pool and be alone with her thoughts for a while and hope, when she returned to the house, her father would not continue with his accusations. For one mad moment she considered going to Simon and asking his advice, but she knew he would insist she stayed and that was impossible. Not because of the trouble it would cause, but because she knew she had to stay well away from Ross Pendennis. Hard work would keep him out of her mind, but to see him and remember the concern in his eyes as he stood beside the bed, the tender kiss he had brushed across her lips before leaving, would break down all her resolves and reawaken the ache in her heart she must not acknowledge.

The drums began as she reached the edge of the village.

Lani stirred and began to stretch as Ross finished dressing. Like a cat, he thought, watching the long, slender hands with their long nails curl and flex. A deadly, dangerous animal of the jungle.

'Where are you going?' She raised herself up on one elbow and stared at him, her eyes narrowing sharply as she realised he was leaving.

'I have some paperwork to catch up on, besides there's going to be bad weather tonight. I might be needed.'

'They know where to find you.' To his surprise she did not begin the usual scene to make him change his mind and stay. She relaxed back on the bed again, stretching languidly beneath the silk sheets he had brought her from San Francisco, every movement designed to make him aware of her body beneath them. 'Are you going to the *haolewahine*?'

'That's a damned stupid question and you know it,' he snapped. She laughed at his indignation.

'If it isn't true why are you angry I asked? I think you would like to have her. Do you think she would satisfy you as much as I do?'

'She might not talk so much which would be a pleasant change,' Ross returned, with a wry smile.

'I have been told how worried you were the night of the fire when she was hurt. Have you slept with her too?'

'She isn't that kind of woman.' Ross pulled on his boots and stood up. The light from the wall torch slanted across his face and she saw the eyes were as hard as black flints. So, she had touched a raw nerve after all.

'Oh, dear. How boring for you.'

She watched him light one of the long cigars he always smoked, thinking of the house she would one day live in, the house he had denied to her. One day soon! He would learn that those who ridiculed Lani, Princess of Wameia, paid a high price for their stupidity. No one would save him from her wrath, not even Tamori. He would be the first to go when the time came, then the *haolewahine* and the old man and she would make this man watch and suffer. When his turn came, his death would be slow and painful and she would enjoy every moment of his agony.

'You look like the cat who's just stolen the cream,' Ross remarked, not liking the gleam in her eyes. Why was there no jealous outburst if she really thought he was going to see Mary Kate? It was the usual pattern of things. It was almost as if she was relieved he was going early. Perhaps Kalakui was back in favour, he thought, not knowing how close he was to the truth.

'When will I see you again?'

'A day or two. I'm sure you can find something to occupy yourself until then,' he flung back over his shoulder as he left her. She uttered a string of unpleasantries after his departing figure, sprang from the bed and called for her maids to come and dress her. She had a more important meeting, which wiped the insult of Ross' departure from her mind for that moment.

'Leaving already?' Tamori grinned at the figure who paused before the verandah to wish him goodnight. He was lounging on a mass of cushions, with two of his favourite wives beside him. 'Are my sister's charms deserting her?'

Ross looked significantly up at the darkening sky. It would rain within the hour, he surmised.

'I have things to do.' His bad humour disappeared as he mounted the steps and crouched beside his friend. 'I can hear the drums. Why?'

'You should know better than to ask, my friend. Go home, Ross, and forget you hear them.'

'I thought you were trying to stop it. If the preacher finds out he'll be over here tomorrow threatening hell-fire and damnation. There'll be one enormous row and it will start a chain of unpleasant events you may not be able to control.'

'Are you expecting me to go against the high priest? You forget he was chosen by Kamehameha himself and is answerable only to him. I am merely the governor of this district. His word is law, you know that. He speaks for the King.'

'And takes another life in his name too?' Ross said in open disgust. He reached for the jug of *awa* at Tamori's side and took a long swallow. 'It makes me sick. I could take some of my men and go and stop it.'

'Then you will surely die. You are my *aikane*—my friend. Listen to my words. It will end, but not in the space of one moon, or two. You must be patient as the *haoles* must be. Kalakui has a strong following. Have you not enough trouble with my sister?'

'What is that supposed to mean?'

'I hear you have eyes for the *haolewahine* lately,' Tamori said and one of his wives giggled behind her hand at the suggestion.

'Not you too,' Ross groaned. 'I help her out with this schoolhouse and everyone's ready to put us beneath the *tapa*. No way, Tamori. Have you been feeding the poison to Lani?'

'She has eyes and ears all over the village. I do not have to say a word. My sister does not like to let go of anything she has owned. She would destroy, rather than relinquish possession. Take care. She could make life very difficult for you.'

'I can take care of myself.' Ross drew thoughtfully on his cigar.

'Of course, but the red headed woman could be in danger. If you care nothing for her, it is of no importance, but if you are taken with her and Lani knows it . . .'

'Taken? With Miss Strait-Laced Purity Whitney?' Ross chuckled aloud at the idea. 'Heaven forbid!'

'Your eyes follow her. Many times I have seen them do so myself.' Tamori helped himself to a drink, belched loudly and offered it to his friend, but Ross shook his head.

'She's not bad to look at,' he admitted reluctantly, 'but taken with her? That little innocent! By all your gods, Tamori, the women here could teach her a thing or two.'

'Convert those who came to convert us? I would like to see that. Do not worry, I will speak to my sister and tell her how displeased I would be if anything happened to the *haolewahine*.'

'No, I'll deal with it myself and I'll start by keeping well away from Miss Mary Kate Whitney, before her father starts getting the same ideas as Lani.'

CHAPTER
EIGHT

THE SOUND of the drums grew louder as Mary Kate approached the pool. It was growing dark, but so far the gathering clouds had not completely obliterated the sky and it was light enough for her to see her way.

As usual whenever she came to this place, she felt a great peace descend over her. She did not want to go back to the house, although it was growing late, to face more of her father's unfounded suspicions. How he must hate her to think such wicked things of her. The rebellious urge to linger until it suited her to return fought against the natural tendency of obedience which had ruled her life since early childhood. Her father's word had always been law to all his family. Mother, son and daughter. One was dead, the other had run away. Now she, herself, at last realised the chains which bound her to a man who cared nothing for her and sought to cast them off.

Moonlight began to filter through the trees around her, slanting across the flowers which grew at the side of the water. To her delight as she watched, the petals began slowly to open, revealing the inside tip of the white flowers were stained with red. Unable to resist their attraction, she picked one and slipped it into her hair, as she had seen many of the island women do. Of course she would remove it before she went home. No sense in giving her father more fuel for his fire. Flowers which needed only the faintest touch of moonlight on them to bloom, instead of the warmth of the sun. Moonflowers! Was that how Ross had come to choose the name for his new ship? It would be appropriate with Pele as a figurehead, for this was her 'special place'.

She caught a sudden movement in the shadows beyond and caught her breath. Someone was watching her!

'Who is it? Who's there?' Even before she received an answer, the glow of a cigar told her the man's identity.

'Don't be alarmed.' Ross came around the pool and stood looking down at her. She was aware of his eyes immediately fastening on the flower in her hair. 'I see the "chosen one of Pele" has found not only her sacred place, but her flowers too.'

'Moonflowers,' Mary Kate said, touching the soft petals. 'I have never seen anything so beautiful.'

'They have a perfect setting. They only bloom when the moon is full, that's why you haven't seen them like this before.'

For a moment his words and the implication behind them were lost on her. Then, bright colour began to rise unbidden in her cheeks. How glad she was of the darkness.

'You know I have been here before? How?'

'Did you find it yourself or did someone show you? Kiki for instance?'

'She did, but I had discovered it already for myself one day when I was out walking.'

'Ah, yes, you like to walk.' Tossing his cigar into the water, Ross sat down beside her. He had told Tamori in all seriousness that he would stay away from this girl, yet not an hour later he found himself with her again and in no hurry to be on his way, even though he knew he should. He would see her safely home first. Not only the weather was unpredictable tonight. Other, more dangerous forces were abroad. 'She forgot to mention this is a short cut to the house and that I use it often?'

'Yes, she did. I'm sorry if my presence here disturbs you, I will leave.'

His hand fastened over hers as she began to rise.

'Stay. Tell me how the school is coming along?'

'Very well.' His fingers caressed the back of her hand and he laughed as she pulled it away. If he was on his way home then he had just left the Princess, Mary Kate suspected, and here he was flirting with her. What kind of man was he? Had he no scruples? 'In a week, perhaps less, I shall be able to hold my first class and the Sunday after, we shall hold services.'

'God forbid,' Ross ejaculated irreverently. 'They aren't ready for the whole hog yet, you know.'

'Father is sure he can persuade Prince Tamori to come to classes and bring his wives. If that happened, the villagers would not be so hesitant to learn,' she continued, ignoring the rude interruption. 'A little prayer might not do you any harm, Captain.'

'Nor would it do me any good. I'm too far gone for redemption, unless of course, you would like to take personal charge of this sinner? You will risk being converted yourself, I might add. Some vices can be quite pleasant, you know. "Ah, make the most of what we may yet spend, before we too into the dust descend. Dust into dust and under dust to lie, *sans* wine, *sans* song, *sans* singer and—*sans* end." A rather apt quotation on my life from one of my favourite writers, Omar Khayyám.'

'I don't think I have ever heard of him,' Mary Kate said, astonished by such eloquence. Never would she have considered Ross Pendennis a man who gained pleasure from books. As he leaned towards her she saw wicked lights dancing in the black eyes.

'Your father would not think him suitable reading for an innocent mind. He was a Persian poet, born about the middle of the eleventh century. He was also quite an astronomer, which is how I first became interested in him. I have a book of his poems at the house if you would care to read them. You might find his philosophy on life interesting, if not challenging.'

'I think not. I am sure I would not appreciate them half as much as you do, Captain. Do you read a great deal?'

'I have the most lurid of tastes. Is that what you wanted to hear?' he retorted mockingly.

'Of course not. I have never thought of you as a man who would find comfort in a book.' More in a woman's arms, she almost added and stopped herself in time. How badly she expressed herself whenever they were together. She tried to be dignified, aloof, and failed. For every time she looked into his eyes she remembered all too vividly the feel of his arms about her, the fierce pressure of his mouth on hers and because she had liked it and wanted it again and hated herself for being so weak, her composure crumpled within a few minutes of being at his side.

'Comfort? Now that's something I've never sought. Knowledge, but never comfort. Enjoyment too, but I've never found the need to shut myself away with a book in order to keep the outside world at bay. Is that how you protect yourself from all that is worldly, Firehair?'

His assessment could not have been more accurate and she had no words to answer him. Leaning closer, he entwined a lock of her loose hair around his fingers and tugged gently. 'Open your eyes. The world about you isn't as bad as you think. I don't believe you can have hair of fire and a heart of ice. The two just don't go together. I know when I kissed you, you enjoyed it, whatever you say to the contrary.'

Mary Kate began to feel quite alarmed as his piratical features came closer. She could not move away for he had tightened his hold on her hair. If anyone came upon them so close together on the grass and told her father . . . ! He would believe all his suspicions to be true and would never forgive her. Nothing she could say would ever make him trust her again.

'Please, I must go. It is late,' she protested. His eyes narrowed as he caught the hesitation in her voice and knew she was afraid. Please, don't let him kiss me, she prayed. I want him to so much, but he mustn't. 'It is not right to be here with you like this,' she protested again when he made no move to release her.

'Why do I bother you so much?' Ross drawled slowly. 'Is it because there is a woman beneath that prim, holier-than-thou attitude, just begging to be released?'

'Don't talk to me like that. It's sinful.'

'For a man to want a beautiful woman? In heaven's name, why did God put them on earth then?'

'You don't believe in God, remember,' Mary Kate flung back and the moon passing into thick cloud, obscured his features as he answered so that she did not see the bitterness openly displayed there.

'I believed in many things once. You remind me of my mother in some ways. In the beginning she was demure and self-righteous too, but it was only a mask with her, worn when my father was about, discarded the moment he went to sea. But I saw it. I've never forgotten how she changed as soon as he had sailed, or the men she took to her bed in his place . . .' He broke off and she sensed a change in him which frightened her more than those hate-filled words.

As she felt his hands slide over her shoulders, Mary Kate knew she had to get away from him before he held her tight and forced more kisses on her unwilling mouth as he had done that day at the house. Surely he did not think that she—He could not! Were all men so intent on fulfilling their own desires they gave no thought to the feelings of the woman herself? Were they mere chattels to be used and then discarded or tolerated until their usefulness was over? She made the mistake of looking into his eyes hoping to find an answer there and she was lost. The intensity of the desire there made her senses swim. No man had ever looked at her this way before.

In that moment of hesitation, Ross's arms closed around her, holding her immobile. He was determined it was not going to be like the last time when she had fled from him in tears. This time he would not allow her to run until he had finished with her and proved to them both that she was exactly what he thought she was. His words to Tamori were forgotten at the touch of her softness against him. The sound of the drums in the background faded from his hearing. He could do nothing in that direction and he would be a fool to interfere—and a very dead one by morning.

'No! No!' Mary Kate's hands moved upwards to exert pressure against his chest, but to no avail.

The protest was silenced as he crushed her mouth beneath his, exploring it with the expertise gained from associations with various women since his first trip to sea with his father at the age of sixteen. There were many tricks he could recall to mind most useful in making a woman more susceptible to seduction. He was startled to discover none were necessary with Mary Kate.

The demanding kisses rained on her face and throat drained from Mary Kate the feeling of shame she had experienced before. If this was wrong, sinful, then her soul was heading for damnation. She never wanted the moment to end. It was the magic dreams were made of. If she was indeed dreaming, she never wanted to awaken, she thought as Ross pressed her back on to the grass, his body hard against hers.

'Hair of fire and heart of ice,' he whispered between the kisses pressed against her cheek. 'I must have been blind. You are warm and alive!'

She moaned softly and thinking she was about to try and free herself, he renewed his determined attack on her unresisting mouth. And then, without warning, he felt a change in her and sensed surrender was almost his. Her body became pliant beneath his hands, no longer tensing each time they attempted a caress. Her lips parted, answering his kiss for kiss, not in the avid way Lani did, but with a childish eagerness he knew could only stem from lack of knowledge.

It was as if a huge chasm had opened up beneath Mary Kate, and she was falling, falling, but she did not mind because Ross was holding her. She had no defence against his greater knowledge, nor against the ache in her heart which cried out to be satisfied. The love she felt for this man was the most wonderful thing that had ever happened to her. No one could ever take it away, or destroy it. If only she could find the words to tell him what was in her heart, but he would not take his mouth from hers.

'Ross.' His name broke from her lips on a soft sigh of pleasure. It was what stopped him before it was too late.

Before he took what she offered—after he had deliberately brought her to the point of surrender—and completed the most cold-blooded seduction of his entire life. He drew back and was shocked to find his hands were shaking. 'What is it?'

Her large eyes were open wide, her mouth bruised and quivering from the onslaught of kisses. She lay still, watching him, desirable beyond his wildest imagination and he knew he must not, could not touch her! Disgust flowed over him like a tidal wave. As it receded, Mary Kate saw his expression alter. The tenderness was wiped from his face as if it had been a mask. She did not like the ugliness beneath.

He stood up and then reached down to pull her to her feet. The moonflower which had fallen from her hair and been crushed beneath them, lay unnoticed on the ground. His grip was so fierce she winced in pain and when he released her, the imprint of his fingers had marked her soft skin.

'Ross.' She said again, not understanding. He did not answer and the realisation something was terribly wrong at last penetrated her mind, shattering the idyllic moment. With it came the knowledge of how close she had come to giving herself to him, she who had known a man's arms about her only once. Only one man's kiss—his! 'What is it?' she repeated, her voice sounded hollow and unreal. The glade was suddenly as cold and unfriendly as the man before her and she ran her hands over her arms, barely able to suppress a shudder. The drums still sounded somewhere behind them. How strange she had not noticed them while she had been in his embrace.

'I don't feel like finishing the game, that's all,' Ross said with a slow smile and the old mockery was back in his voice to brutally complete the destruction of a dream.

'Game? I don't understand.'

'I wanted you. It's that simple. As you wanted me to kiss you that other time.' He knew he had to be without pity, destroy that moment they had just shared so that it never happened again. He had to make her hate him. 'I was playing a game with you, girl, don't you realise that? I have been all along. Lani has been difficult these past weeks and I was using you to bring her back into line.'

If he had struck her with all his might, it would have hurt her less than those words. Mary Kate took a step backwards. Her lips moved, but no sound came. No condemnation, nothing. Not even tears. He had been prepared for both, wanted them for they would have been easier to ridicule and dismiss with more spiteful rhetoric. Her eyes spoke for her. Those lovely sapphire eyes contained horror and revulsion and soul-rending misery so terrible to see it took all his self-control not to pull her back into his arms and confess what had happened to him in that short time.

'Didn't you hear me?' Damn her, why didn't she fly at him? Scream, shout, use her nails on his face as Lani had once done when he ignored her. She had not attempted it a second time! 'It was a game. A few stolen kisses mean nothing to a man, don't you know that? I was amusing myself with you.'

As her father had predicted. More pain! Would it never end?

'Why did you stop?' Her voice was low, but perfectly controlled. She was like a Grecian statue, he thought, made of white alabaster. Beautiful to look at, but cold and unobtainable. He had achieved his aim. It gave him little satisfaction.

The question offered the opportunity he sought and he used it ruthlessly, with no regard to her feelings or his own. Pushing his hands deep into his pockets, he gave her an ugly smile.

'You are not Lani.' He laid heavy emphasis on the words and saw by the way she winced that no more were necessary.

'May God forgive you, for I never will,' Mary Kate said and her voice faltered and broke.

With the dignity of a queen, she walked away and left him. She heard him swear as she reached the pathway and the first tears blinded her vision, but she did not look back. She quickened her footsteps, not realising the curses were not meant for her.

Mary Kate paused at a section of the path which came out of the trees and overlooked the village to get her bearings. In the darkness she was afraid of wandering for miles in the wrong direction. The moon was still in cloud, the sky black and starless. A sharp breeze whipped her hair into wild disorder about her wet cheeks. She brushed a hand across her face. She felt cold and was trembling violently. He had treated her like a whore! She had given him no cause for that. Conflicting emotions rampaged through her. Love, hate, shock, coupled with the agonising feeling of rejection. She had offered herself, all she had, and he had laughed at her because she was not as skilled as his mistress. A child in his eyes, not a woman at all. She knew nothing of love. It was not wonderful. She wondered if the feeling of shame engulfing her would ever go away.

How those drums throbbed. It was a slow, monotonous beat which never altered. Over and over again. Boom! Boom! Boom! Some kind of signal, she wondered, a warning of the bad weather almost upon them? She could feel the first spots of rain on her face and looked desperately around for some landmark, a light.

What was that flickering amid the trees? Torches? But it was not the village. The lights were moving. She counted ten in all, moving slowly up the slopes not a hundred yards away. A procession of some kind? They seemed to be moving in the direction of the drumbeats, coming from the dense undergrowth which lay in the direction of the mountains.

Her eyes fixed stolidly on the flickering lights, she began to move towards them, stumbling over uneven ground in the blackness and barely unable to hold back a cry of pain as her bandaged hands sought guidance from the ferns about her and found the pain too great to do so. She did not know where they were going, but they had to come from the village. Somewhere over there was the path home. Her father would be frantic with worry—or would he?

She paused again for breath, the headlong flight from the pool had left her with very little and the ground was difficult to negotiate with a strong wind continually buffeting her, whipping her skirts about her legs and threatening to topple her over if she did not concentrate every moment. Her assumption had been correct. She could now see the pole torches erected in the centre of the village and the outline of several huts. She was almost home. Wait, more torches, coming up to meet her. She was caught between two lines of people.

'Get down, girl. For God's sake, they mustn't see you,' a voice hissed directly behind her and she almost fainted with fright. He had followed her! Had he changed his mind and decided she might provide him with a little amusement after all? Unceremoniously Ross pulled her backwards into the heavy foliage. 'Be still and quiet and pray they go straight past us. And I do mean pray.'

'Let me go. Are you mad? Haven't you done enough to me for one night?' Mary Kate scathed, twisting around in his grasp to glare at him. 'Go to Lani for your fun, I won't provide it for you.'

He was holding her down by the weight of his body thrown across hers, his hands grasping her shoulders in an exceedingly painful grip. The face that loomed close to hers was grim and frightening.

'Be still, you little fool or I'll knock you cold. One sound and both our lives will be in danger. Do you understand that?'

'Why? Where are those people going? Tell me . . .'

A hand abruptly covered her mouth, shutting off her questions. Mary Kate squirmed in indignation beneath its confines. His skin smelt of tobacco. He only increased the pressure of his fingers until his hold was so uncomfortable she became still.

More drums, close at hand this time. Ross was watching the approaching *kanakas* through narrowed eyes. Kalakui in his feathered cloak and behind him, Lani! He blinked and looked again. Yes, it was her and dressed in the regalia of one of the sacred women, chosen by the high-priest to officiate in the temple at his side. So that was the way of it. No wonder she had not cared that he left her early. Had he not, she would have had to make some excuse to make him do so. Her presence was demanded tonight and she dared not refuse. He wondered if Tamori knew of his sister's activities. Probably not. Lani kept the laws, paid homage to the gods, but to become a sacred temple woman, meant she would die for the old ways if it was demanded of her. Her life belonged to Ku, the Cruel One. She had kept her secret well. So it was Kalakui and Lani against Tamori. He would stand no chance against the power of the two combined. At least he knew the score, Ross thought, his mouth tightening into a bleak line.

He could hear the *kanakas* moving through the grass and ferns towards them. He flattened himself more over Mary Kate, his face against her cheek. She saw his eyes as he did so and grew terribly afraid. In them she read the truth! The drums meant death! Sacrifice! Human sacrifice!

Her heart almost stopped beating as one man passed so close dirt showered them from the gnarled staff he was using to aid him climb the steep incline. The weight of Ross' body was suffocating, but he did not move and she could not. It seemed an eternity before he withdrew his hand.

His body still held hers prisoner. For a long moment the narrowed eyes stared down into hers. She lay beneath him like a statue, her body tense and frightened as she relived with vivid clarity those moments of ecstasy beside the pool and the rejection and humiliation which followed. Her eyes closed tightly so that he would not see the anguish and misery mirrored there.

'It's safe. They have gone now,' he said at length and eased himself away from her.

She brushed aside the hand he offered and struggled to her feet.

'Whether you believe it or not, I've just saved your life. And mine,' he added heavily. And with heavier sarcasm, 'Don't bother to thank me!'

'I—I only have your word that we were in any danger.'

'Oh, we were, Firehair, make no mistake about that. If we had been discovered, there would have been three corpses for the rats tomorrow, instead of one.'

His words chilled her. She lifted her eyes to the torches ahead of them and watched them slowly disappear one by one.

'Where are they going?' she whispered. 'Tell me. I must know.'

'So that you can chase after them and save the poor unfortunate victim? I'll tell you another time. Right now, I'm taking you home where little girls belong.'

He grabbed her arm and began down the slope, jerking her none too gently when her steps faltered. Her questions fell on deaf ears. Her threats were ignored. He answered to neither, but continued to urge her on ruthlessly until they reached the house. By that time it was raining heavily and both of them were soaked to the skin.

'Is your father not here?' he asked, staring at the darkened window. 'Good grief, don't tell me he is out there somewhere too?'

'No . . .' Mary Kate tried the door and found it locked. For a moment she was speechless. He had deliberately shut her out believing she had a clandestine meeting with Ross! Was this night of humiliation to go on forever?

'What is it?' Ross too, tried the door and then wheeled on her with an oath. 'Well, is he in or out?'

'In. I think he has gone to bed. No, don't knock. He won't answer,' she entreated. 'For the love of heaven, just go away and leave me alone.'

'Won't answer? Why?'

'We—we had an argument. It is none of your business.' It had everything to do with him, but he would never know it. Her father was inside listening to every word, she suspected. She had returned with Ross which would confirm his suspicions. She blinked back a rush of tears. She would sleep in the schoolroom on one of the *tapa* mats. She had no other choice. She did not care how uncomfortable it might be so long as she was alone.

'Then I'll break down the door. Dammit! You can't stay out in this weather,' Ross said, in a disbelieving tone.

"I'll spend the night next door. Your concern is not necessary, Captain. Just go!' she begged wearily. She suddenly felt exhausted.

'You'll do no such thing. Either you let me rouse him or you are coming back to the house with me. Of all nights you chose this one to argue with him,' he added in an exasperated tone. 'You'll sleep behind locked doors tonight, my girl.'

'I shall stay here,' she insisted stubbornly.

An ear-splitting clap of thunder made her start violently. The sound reverberated up and down the length of the valley. Never before had she known the elements in such a fury. If she had believed in evil omens, she would have said this was one.

'You are coming with me,' Ross said and his hand fastened over her wrist in a vice-like grip. Struggle as she might, she was dragged after him back to where he had left his horse on the path to the pool.

The fury of the wind increased with each passing moment until it was so strong they were almost swept off their feet on several occasions. By the time he pulled her up in front of him, she was half-fainting with cold and fear and she knew little of the journey to the house.

When she awoke next morning, still wrapped in the voluminous robe Mamalou had given her, the sun was streaming through the windows on to the bed and it was as if the storm had been no more than a bad dream. A nightmare, she thought, as she lay there remembering all that had happened. Ross with her beside the pool, the *kanakas* going to take part in a blood sacrifice, the locked door which barred her from her own home and the appalling ride afterwards. It would be a long time before she forgot any of it.

She climbed out of bed and went downstairs to find Mamalou and her clothes, knowing she must quickly return to her father before she added to the felony of disobedience by staying away still longer. It was unthinkable that she should remain beneath the roof of Ross Pendennis, destroyer of her love, which is what Simon had insisted she must do as soon as he was told what had occurred. He would not have been so eager had he known the rest, she thought as she descended the stairs, but she knew she could not confide in him. It was a cross she would bear alone and in silence.

They were all seated at the table eating breakfast as she hesitantly looked into the kitchen. One glance was all Ross gave her before he continued with his food.

'Mary Kate, good heavens, I thought you would sleep until noon after Mamalou's herbal tea,' Simon exclaimed, climbing to his feet to pull out a chair for her. 'Sit down and have some coffee and something to eat. You don't look any the worse the wear for your unpleasant experience, does she Ross?'

Which one, was the question in Mary Kate's eyes as her gaze encountered that of Ross.

'Only coffee. Thank you. I'm not at all hungry. If my clothes are dry, I really must go home.'

'Oh, no,' Kiki said, her expression registering disappointment. 'Simon said you might stay.'

'He had no right to say that. I did not agree. You know

I can't leave Father alone in the midst of all this work, Simon. He needs me. He will be worrying where I am,' she protested. 'I have to go back.'

She felt Ross's eyes on her, did not look up from her coffee. Liar, they would be silently saying. He cares as little for you as I do.

'I'll have horses saddled and get you home then,' Simon said with a shrug, 'but I wish you'd reconsider. You had a nasty experience last night. As a doctor I suggest you spend a couple of days in bed. When I redressed that one hand I saw it had reopened again. You shouldn't use it. Besides you might have caught a chill.'

'I will take care,' Mary Kate promised. 'Were we really in danger, Simon?' How sweet he was to worry so. It eased a little of the pain inside her.

Ross's gaze was on her instantly, angrily, and she quickly looked away.

"Did you think I was joking?' he demanded tersely and everyone, except her, stared at him surprised by his tone. 'Only a chosen few attend those ceremonies, the remainder of the village stay indoors on pain of death if they venture outside. For you to have seen the faces of those going to the temple would have meant certain death, or if you had been caught watching.'

'You saw them,' she said. He had placed his life in danger to save her! She quickly squashed a brief moment of pity. He had afforded her none beside the pool. She would give none.

'Not for the first time and Kalakui knows it. If you hear the drums again, shut yourself in the house and don't come out until morning, is that clear?'

Mamalou nodded agreement, her face grave.

'But where were they going?' she insisted.

'You will have nightmares if I tell you,' came the dry retort and it was then Simon intervened.

'She's not a child, Ross. Tell her.'

'Curiosity in these parts can lead to sudden death,' Ross warned and saw her pale visibly. 'Kalakui was taking them to the temple of Ku, the Cruel One. There, they sacrificed the young girl who was with them. The temple is an ugly old place in the shadow of the Big Mountain. God knows how many unfortunates have met their death there. Inside is a huge chasm in the floor, probably the result of past volcanic activity. The sacrifices are thrown into it. I've been told it's bottomless. I've seen it and I believe it. You asked to be told,' he snapped as Mary Kate's hands flew to her mouth.

'I have to know what we are up against. What we have to fight,' she answered, determined to stay in control of herself. The way he looked at her, spoke to her, it was as if last night had never happened. How could he have held her in his arms, kissed her so ardently and now stare at her across the table as if she was a stranger? 'Can the Prince not stop them? These sacrifices?'

'The high priest is answerable only to the King,' Simon said quietly. Tamori is powerless to prevent them and don't forget Kamehameha still conforms to the old ways. He is too old to change now.'

'How—how often do these rituals take place?' She ignored the warning look thrown at her by Ross. She had to know everything, however unpleasant.

'Whenever one of the gods needs appeasing or Kalakui feels the need to arouse the people,' he said, tight-lipped. 'Last night I suspect the girl he sacrificed was intended to be a peace offering. Tribute from the faithful followers of Ku. Including the Princess Lani.'

'Good God,' Simon said, startled. Mamalou and Kiki

exchanged anxious glances. It was obvious they had not known before and the news was worrying.

'Today Kalakui will be telling everyone Ku is not satisfied,' Ross continued. 'He is still angry at the strangers in his midst, hence the length of the storm and the destruction it has no doubt caused.'

'Strangers? Do you mean us?' Mary Kate demanded, anger rising inside her at such a suggestion. Kalakui would use the ignorance of the people to full advantage.

'I could be wrong, but I know how his mind works. I fear, and I mean fear, an alliance between Kalakui and Lani against her brother.'

'What will that mean?'

'Bloodshed, child,' Mamalou replied, solemnly. 'Yours perhaps, mine, Ross's. Terrible bloodshed.'

'If only Tamori was not so weak,' Simon interposed. 'We might stand a chance of rousing the younger people, to side with us.'

'You could do that,' Mary Kate challenged Ross with her words. 'If you love this place as much as you say you do, isn't it worth fighting for?'

She heard Kiki beside her give a gasp as without a word, Ross rose from the table and strode from the room.

'He was twenty when he saw his first tribal warfare,' Mamalou said, in a disapproving voice. 'Tamori's uncle tried to seize power when his father died. It went on for two weeks only. Bloody battles that left whole families dead. I lost my sister and brother who had come to live in the village from Honolulu. Children were left without parents or relatives. That is why there are so few old people here. He does not want to see it again. It tore him apart. The chasm in Ku's temple stank with rotting flesh for months afterwards. That is how captured prisoners are disposed of here too. One of those who died was Ross's own father! Your clothes will be dry now. Will you fetch them, Kiki.'

'Mamalou,' Simon said quietly, 'I would like to speak to my sister alone for a moment. Would you mind?'

When they were alone, Simon turned on Mary Kate, his young face deeply disturbed.

'Before I take you back I want the answers to some questions. Ross said you told him there had been an argument with Father and that was why you were locked out. Since when did you ever stand up against him?'

'That isn't fair,' she gasped. 'I took your side often enough before you left home and I always defended you afterwards. Even now, living with Kiki, refusing to acknowledge your own father, I still defend you, because I love you. And I have come to love her as a sister. Don't you understand all I want to do is to get us together again? All of us.'

'Was that the reason?'

'Yes—and no. I don't want to go into detail, Simon. I said things to him of which I am very ashamed. I have to go back and apologise and remember we have to work together if we are to achieve anything here. That is more important than petty squabbles.'

'Was Ross's name mentioned by any chance?' Simon watched the colour drain from her face. She had been barely conscious when the latter had carried her into the house, both soaking wet and badly frightened. With good reason, he realised afterwards when he learned what had taken place. But he had also seen the way his sister looked at Ross as he sat at the table this morning and the expression in her eyes puzzled him. What had happened to the friendship beginning to spring up between them? Something else had happened which neither wished to discuss and he felt concerned at the mark it had left on her.

'Why do you ask that?' Her voice faltered nervously. 'Why should it?'

'Every visit Father has made to Tamori, he has spoken out against Ross. His way of living, his relationship with Lani, as if Ross is the thing he must destroy, not Kalakui and his graven idols. He's even accused him of trying to corrupt you. He is treading a dangerous path.'

'Does Ross . . .' Quickly she corrected herself. She would never say that hated name again, 'the Captain know?'

'Yes. Tamori is his friend. They grew up together as young men. Don't you see you are being used, Mary Kate, as I was? As Mother was?'

'That will not happen. Father knows I have a mind of my own now. He may not like it, but he will not rule my life the way he did before. I stay because I want to and for no other reason.'

'Once I was the favourite, do you remember?' Simon asked, with a bitter smile. 'I never understood why because you and Mother tried so hard to please him. Only I seemed to succeed. I was seventeen before I discovered why. I told him I wanted to become a doctor. He said that was not possible as I was going to follow in his footsteps and become a preacher. I would succeed where he had failed because I had the ability to reach out and touch people's hearts. Do you know what that did to me? He had been a failure all his life and so I was to take his place and make up for all those lost dreams and ambitions. I was a sacrifice to his personal vanity. As you will be if you don't break away from him now. Come and live here with us. Ross would welcome you, I know it and Kiki and Mamalou.'

'What you ask is impossible,' Mary Kate said, quickly rising to her feet.

'Because of what happened between you and Ross last night? I don't know what it was, only that he is like a bear with a sore head this morning and you can't look him in the eyes.'

'Nothing happened,' his sister replied through trembling lips and knew she had not deceived him for a moment. 'I will go and get ready to go home.'

CHAPTER
NINE

THE opening of the schoolroom two days after Mary
Kate's return to the village far surpassed her expectations. With Kiki accompanying her she had gone from
hut to hut the day before asking the women to come and
bring their children, and had been pleased with the
reception she received. Only a few had dismissed the
suggestion out of hand.

The next morning, although she was ready at eight
o'clock, no one appeared until just before ten. Nuina
and her three children. Slowly they began to creep into
the hut and sit down on the *tapa* mats to watch the
haolewahine write the strange new writing on the huge
blackboard. Mary Kate's hopes for success rose when
Tamori appeared, together with a servant to fan him
with a *kahili* to keep away the flies, another with a jug of
awa which he fed his royal master at regular intervals
and his two favourite wives who were very young, pretty
and extremely fat. They giggled and whispered behind
their hands to each other for most of the morning, but
she did not mind. The Prince had put his seal of approval
on the school of 'new learning', as he called it. Where he
went, others would follow.

She was to discover, as the days passed, however, that
Tamori only appeared when the fancy took him and was
thankful the others did not follow his example. He had
left strict instructions they were to remain and learn,

Kiki told her, also jubilant at the unexpected success they had achieved.

The Sunday prayers, conducted by her father, were not regarded in the same vein. The people liked to sit and listen to the soft voice of the 'chosen one of Pele', Kiki explained one evening after only three people had appeared for the Sunday service, but not to the angry roar of the 'whiskered one', which was how they spoke of Nathaniel. They regarded his teachings to be little different from those of the high priest. If they offended the new God, they would be cast into the eternal fires of hell, they were told. If they offended their own gods they would die, Kalakui warned. They saw no difference, so why should they change the old gods for a new one who offered them nothing better?

Simon would have made them listen, Mary Kate thought, a trifle sadly. Now she knew how desperately her father wanted him back. She had not allowed her brother to remain with her once she had returned home, but the reception which greeted her was far different from the one she had been expecting and dreading. Nathaniel, working with the *kanakas* inside the schoolroom, looked up as she entered, but said nothing. He was going to make it as difficult for her as possible, she had thought, but he did not.

'You are back then?' Was all he said as she braced herself for the initial onslaught of his temper. He did not sound in the least angry.

'Yes, Father.'

'You will not continue this relationship with Captain Pendennis?' he continued, moving towards her, his eyes fixed on her ashen cheeks.

'What I thought to be friendship, he considered something else,' Mary Kate replied. She owed him that much of an explanation. 'I will not see him again, nor speak to him unless it is necessary. I did not—not spend the night with him, you have to believe that.'

'He brought you home.'

So he had heard, or seen them outside in the teeming rain and still not unlocked the door! How unfeeling he was. At first she had not understood the lack of anger, now she did. She had come back. Their work—his work, would go on with her at his side as he had always intended. If he felt anything for what had happened to her it would not be pity, or regret, but satisfaction.

'Something terrible happened last night. On my way back here I saw people going towards the mountains with torches.' She gave a detailed explanation of the procession and who had been in it and saw anger begin to burn in Nathaniel's eyes. If she had stayed the night with Ross, she suspected this news would have taken precedence over it. 'That was why the Captain brought me home. He saved my life.'

'Yet he did nothing to stop the murder of an innocent young girl. The man is beyond God's mercy. I must go and see the Prince immediately and inform him of this.'

'He knows, Father, but he does not have Kalakui's following. He can do nothing.'

'He allows his own sister to participate in the taking of a human life?' Nathaniel echoed, his voice rising sharply. Several of the *kanakas* looked at him warily as they worked. 'It is unthinkable. How does the Captain know so much?'

'He has lived here since he was fifteen, Father, he has seen it all before, I suppose. But what could he do, one man alone?'

'Stand fast to all that is good and decent, yet he consorts with that jezebel Princess openly and without shame, knowing the kind of woman she is.'

'I don't think he knew about her being a temple priestess until last night,' Mary Kate said and her father's flint-grey eyes narrowed in her direction.

'You defend him?' he thundered and she shook her head, not answering.

He left her to continue making the schoolroom ready, sorting through the writing books and others they had brought in readiness for this day. Returning just before dark, he calmly informed her he had challenged the authority of Kalakui, by threatening him with the wrath of the Almighty if he did not cease his barbaric practices and Tamori too, had spoken up against them. Mary Kate was both elated and apprehensive at the news. For the Prince to make a stand with her father was a major victory, but had it been wise? How could he, without a sufficient number of men prepared to fight for him, hope to continue in defiance of all he had once believed in? And how would Kalakui react to such a threat to his power? That was what really worried her.

She did not have to wait long for the answer. It happened one night as they were eating supper. The sudden sound of snapping wood made Mary Kate run to the window. She cried out at the sight of their precious books being thrown into the dust, where a *kanaka* waited with a flaming torch to set them alight. Six, perhaps seven other men were wielding axes against the flimsy bamboo walls, pulling at the straw on the roof. Another few minutes and there would be nothing left!

'Father, they are wrecking the school!' she cried.

Nathaniel reached the door before her, bellowing like a bull enraged at what he saw. He showed no fear as he ran to the gate and flung it open and advanced towards the nearest man who turned, brandishing a gleaming two-bladed axe. It was never used. Seeing who faced him, the man gave him a powerful thrust which sent him reeling backwards to the ground where he lay half-stunned. Like shadows, the men turned and disappeared into the trees.

Kalakui had won the first round, Mary Kate thought as she bathed her father's bruised cheek and made a cup of tea for them both, after an inspection of the damage. She had seen enough of his hideously tattooed followers to know who had sent the men to cause the destruction. She suspected they had orders not to go beyond that, for her father could easily have been killed. It had been meant as a warning. She said as much as Nathaniel began speaking of the rebuilding.

'A bamboo hut,' Nathaniel was not impressed by her misgivings. 'It can be rebuilt. We will buy more writing materials. If we cannot afford them I will go to the Prince. He should have foreseen this.'

'Do you really believe Kalakui will stop at the wrecking of the hut? I don't. No one came to our aid tonight, didn't you realise that? We stand alone in this.'

'We are not alone, we are within the sight of God. Under His protection. Tomorrow you will send that woman Nuina, to Simon, tell him we need men again.'

He would hear no more said on the matter and went to bed. Mary Kate failed to sleep at all that night.

They did not have to send word to Simon. The appearance of Ross early the next morning proved the news had travelled fast. It was the first time she had seen him since he walked out on her at breakfast that day at the house. She had no chance to avoid him for she was kneeling in the dirt trying to salvage what was left of the burnt and scorched books when a shadow fell across her and looking up, she found him looming over her.

'I heard what happened,' he said with a frown. 'Where is your father, I must speak with him?'

'He went to see the Prince. He has some foolish notion Tamori will be able to stop Kalakui. We both know he won't, don't we, Captain?'

The bitterness in her tone stung him. Damn her, how had she managed to get under his skin? He had guarded himself so well, yet she was there, day and night continually to torment him. Her lovely eyes looked tired and he surmised she had not slept after the school had been wrecked. One of her hands was still bandaged, but the other was not and he saw faint white scars across the softly tanned palm, reminding him of how she had risked her life to save a child. The life which was in danger again because of her father's stupid challenge to the most powerful man in the area. He knew Kalakui would kill them without hesitation if he did not find some way to prevent it. The question was how? They would refuse the protection he offered and he could not have them watched night and day, he did not have sufficient men brave enough to risk the anger of the gods by going against their high priest.

He could ask Tamori to make them return to Honolulu. That was their only chance. They would not thank him for it, but at least they would be alive. Of course, to get Nathaniel Whitney aboard the *Moonflower* he would probably have to tie him hand and foot, but if that was what it took then he would have it done and he knew Simon would back him.

'What do you want, Captain? You are not welcome here.'

'You have made that very plain. I came to warn you, though I know now you fully realise the danger you are in. You must leave here immediately, go back to

Honolulu. I will take you as soon as you are packed,' he said harshly and her eyes widened in disbelief at the suggestion.

'We have no intention of leaving. That would be admitting defeat.' Another failure for her father. He would never agree to it and if she went alone, left him to whatever Kalakui had in store for them, she would never be able to hold her head up again. She climbed to her feet, wiping the dust from her skirts. Her hair was tied back again in that same uninteresting knot, he saw. She looked weary—somehow older. Had he done this to her?

'Don't tell me you are not afraid, because I know you are,' he said roughly. He had to shake her out of this mistaken sense of loyalty, for he was sure that was all it was. 'Why won't you heed me? Is it because of what happened between us? Forget it! I have.'

Mary Kate's shoulders stiffened visibly. How dare he mentioned that night.

'I have no recollection of anything happening between us, Captain. Please go, before my father returns.'

'Good God, isn't there anything I can say or do to rouse you out of your stupor, make you realise the danger you will be in if Kalakui's men go on the rampage? Perhaps there is. I managed to arouse something in you before, didn't I, Firehair?'

Regardless of who might be watching them, he caught her up in his arms, forced back her head and pressed his lips to hers. There was no response, no softening of the tight mouth beneath his, and he stepped back with an oath.

'The only thing you arouse in me is disgust,' Mary Kate scathed. 'Is the Princess still proving "difficult" that you seek me out again?'

He could have slapped her for the remark and the cold fury which engulfed him, instead he used words to hurt her as he had always done with great success.

'Why, Mary Kate,' he drawled insolently, his eyes glittering with malicious satisfaction as she sensed his intention and sunk her teeth deeply into her lower lip. 'If I didn't know better, I would think you were jealous.'

He remounted his horse and stared down at her, wishing he could abandon her to her fate—little fool, she deserved it—and knowing he could not.

'I'll see the Prince too and try to work something out. Meanwhile I'll have some of my men come back and start repairs. You'll be needing new *tapa* mats and another blackboard, I suppose?' She nodded wordlessly. He shamed her and took great pleasure it in, yet when everyone else abandoned them, he came with more help. She would never understand him, or the love which still remained buried inside her, refusing to be dulled by all he had done. 'You'll have the mats and men in the morning. I'll have to send to Duncan for the rest. Don't thank me, you wouldn't mean it,' came the sarcastic taunt as he rode away and she turned away and went into the house, blinking back hot tears.

For three days Ross's men worked energetically on the schoolroom and during that time Simon and Kiki came to try and persuade her to live with them. As always she refused. In his desperation her brother went inside the house and asked his father to come also, or at least allow Mary Kate to do so. Nathaniel looked at his daughter and said if she wished to leave, she was free to do so, knowing full well she would not. She had inherited her mother's steadfast loyalty. She would not desert him in his hour of need and when it was over she would be bound to him closer than ever before. Not by love, but by what they had endured together. God was testing his faith, his courage, in this final assault upon his beliefs.

'No, Simon,' Mary Kate said quietly, determinedly and he knew she would not change her mind. 'I shall stay here.'

The drums awoke her just after midnight. The same throbbing sound as she had heard the night of the sacrifice. There was to be another, she thought, trying to still the panic rising inside her as she sprang out of bed and pulled on her robe. Who was it to be tonight? Another young girl? Her father? Herself? She had to stay calm, they might not mean that at all, but when she went out into the other room, she found her father was already awake and dressed. He too, feared the worst. He had refused the rifle Simon had offered. How she wished she had taken it and hidden it somewhere. No, it would have been false courage and to take the life of another human being was something her father would not do, even though his own might be at risk.

'Sit down, daughter,' Nathaniel said quietly. 'We will read together.'

Mary Kate stared at him stunned. It could not be God's will that they remained like sheep until Kalakui and his murdering followers came and dragged them away to the temple of Ku and thrust them into the pit. He was like the island gods, demanding sacrifices! Every fibre of her being rebelled at the thought of doing nothing. Her father looked up at her, but before he could speak, the acrid smell of smoke invaded the room. Her eyes flew to the roof and she screamed at the sight of smoke pouring through the straw. It had been set alight.

In a short time the walls would catch fire and they would be trapped.

'Father, quickly,' she caught his arm, dragging him towards the door. Why did he shake her off, did he want to die in a blazing inferno? The memory of that other fire swept over her making her feel sick with fear. The heat, the noise of the flames, the suffocating, choking smoke. Again he shrugged her off.

She pulled at the door. It stuck for an agonising minute before yielding. She reeled back into the room at the sight of the feathered spear which was embedded in the thick wood, the only substantial part of the house there was. Her father was at her side, his eyes almost puzzled as he looked at her.

'It should not happen this way,' he said, shaking his head slowly.

'What, Father?' she asked through trembling lips. She dreaded the answer.

'The manner of our death. They must know why we are willing to give up our lives. If they do not, we have achieved nothing.'

'No! No! You don't know what you are saying. Father, come back,' she cried as he moved past her as if in a dream, slowly down the path towards the gate and the crowd of men who waited. Kalakui, resplendent in his feathered cloak, Lani by his side, her lips parted in a smile of anticipation as she watched the hungry flames licking around the first bamboos. Armed men, whose faces bore no expression. They had seen it all before. And Tamori! Not him too! He had changed sides. There was no hope for them, they would die! Why had she not listened to Ross, to Simon? Why had she allowed her pride to stand in the way of common sense? 'Father, they will not listen . . .'

If he heard her, which she doubted, his steps did not falter. Before Kalakui he stopped and opened the Bible in his hands. She could not hear what he was saying. The voice, so often raised in anger, or passionate outbursts of fervour, was strangely quiet. He was praying, she realised, pressing her hands against her mouth to shut out a cry. The last words of a man prepared to die for what he believed in. There was no fear on his face. In those few moments before Kalakui gave the signal for his men to fall upon Nathaniel Whitney and deliberately and in cold blood, kill him and then mutilate his body, she forgot about the fire threatening her, the threat to her own life, as she fell to her knees and prayed to God in his infinite mercy to save her father from certain death.

The killing frenzy over, the men fell back awaiting their next victim. Mary Kate raised her head and stared at them through eyes streaming with tears. Tears of fear, horror at what she had witnessed, pity for the man who had given up his life in vain. They cared nothing for the gesture. To them, his death was a victory, as hers would be. With the *haoles* dead there would be no more threat to the old ways. If Ross was right, Tamori would be the next to go, leaving Kalakui and Lani to rule in his place, answerable only to Kamehameha.

Ross! He would never know she had loved him, never realise how close she had come to surrender that night. And Simon! He was lucky to have Kiki, she would console him in his loss. Were they in danger too from these blood-thirsty fiends?

Red-hot cinders began to fall from the roof. She backed towards the door, but could not bring herself to turn and run outside. She did not want to die! She tried to pray, but in this greatest hour of need she had ever known, she could not find the words to pray to the God who had allowed her father to be butchered before her very eyes. A huge wall of flame sprang up beside her forcing her out into the open. No one moved as she appeared, her arms shielding her face from the intense heat. This time her appearance caused no reaction.

As she lowered her arms, Kalakui stepped forward, his face twisted into a cruel smile. Lani was watching her brother's face, scornful of the indecision there.

'So the "chosen one of Pele" fears the flames after all.' He looked about him triumphantly. 'Did I not tell you she was an impostor? Pele did not send this white-skinned *haolewahine* to us with words from a new and more powerful God. Who is more powerful than Ku, the Cruel One? Kane, the father of men? Or his brother Kanaloa? Or Pele, who has sent the fire to consume this false one? Take her. Throw her back into the flames. If they do not harm her, I, Kalakui, high priest of Wameia, will do homage to her. I will rub my face in the dirt at her feet and you will follow me. Take her!'

Mary Kate screamed in terror as she was seized by two *kanakas* and turned back towards the blazing hut. She struggled like a madwoman to be free of the grip on her arms and wrists, but against the power of the men who held her, she was like a baby. Tongues of flame were already licking around the doorway. She was dragged bodily back along the path near to fainting. When her legs gave out beneath her, they hauled her upright, preparing to thrust her over the threshold.

The first *kanaka* died with a bullet between his eyes. She did not hear the shot Ross fired from the trees, nor the second one which came from Simon's gun. She could hear nothing but the roar of the flames as she sank to the ground in a crumpled heap.

Behind Ross and Simon there were four more armed

men. Slowly, warily, they advanced towards the crowd of natives. As axes and spears rose menacingly, Ross ordered,

'Tell your men to be still, Kalakui. I have more guns trained on your backs. If you don't believe me, tell them to commit suicide.' His cold gaze centred on Tamori. 'I didn't expect to see you here, but at least I know now the way the wind blows. If you've harmed Mary Kate, I may do a little sacrificing of my own tonight. Cover them, and shoot the first man to move. I don't care who it is.' He ordered his men.

Mary Kate lay face down in the dirt. He felt his heart lurch unsteadily as he turned her over and saw the graze on her cheek where one of the *kanakas* had struck her as she struggled with him. Her pulse was strong beneath his fingers. She was still alive, but what would tonight have done to her mind? To have seen her own father hacked to pieces, been threatened with the agonising death by fire. He picked up her limp form and carried it outside the paling.

'It's all right. She's fainted, that's all,' he reassured Simon who started forward anxiously, and laid her down again. The weapon in his hand came up to menace Kalakui. 'I was never one for reading the Preacher's Bible, but I do know there's a passage in it which says "an eye for an eye and a tooth for a tooth". You took a life tonight, my friend. Why shouldn't I take yours?'

'You will be dead before you can reload. You and your friends and then I will offer Ku another gift.' Kalakui looked significantly towards Mary Kate's unconscious figure. 'It would be pleasant to kill you. I have long looked forward to it.'

'You forget yourself.' Tamori's voice shook with repressed anger as he stepped out of the crowd. 'We did not come to kill. You went against my orders—and for the last time!'

'Why did you come?' Ross enquired quietly. There was nothing he would have liked better than to put a bullet into Kalakui and he knew Simon, at his side, had his finger tightly around the trigger, begging for an excuse to pull it. Knew also, for the few people they might kill, albeit Kalakui and Tamori among them, they themselves would surely die and then Mary Kate would be at the mercy of those fanatics left and that meant the pit in the temple of Ku. 'Why? To challenge the Preacher's God?'

'If he is more powerful, why did he not protect them? The woman was afraid, she did not come from Pele.'

'That makes it easier, does it? What happened to the words we spoke to each other only yesterday? Did Lani come to you afterwards? Did you allow her persuasive tongue to shut your ears to what we had said?'

'I warned you not to interfere,' Tamori interrupted. 'Why are you here? This is no concern of yours?'

'You are wrong, my friend. I have come to protect my woman.' The words were out before he had given them thought. His woman! She had come close to it once and then he had sent her away, berating her with hateful words to shame and hurt her. No, she did not belong to him, yet he felt an overwhelming desire to protect her and knew, although he had never admitted it to himself, it had always been with him since the first moment he realised what a little innocent she was. He could no longer put her into the same category as the other women he had known and made love to and discarded. She was different and he had known it and refused to accept the fact. Had his pride and bitterness not had the controlling vote in his life, he would have taken her to the house when he began to suspect trouble and kept her there by any means necessary. She would not be lying at his feet now under sentence of death, had he done so.

'Your woman?' Lani threw back her head and laughed. 'You lie. She has never belonged to you. Not as I do.'

'Did,' Ross corrected, aware of the constantly changing expressions on Tamori's face. He had come tonight because Kalakui was stronger, but now he had other allies. How he would turn it to his advantage, he did not know, only that the Prince had as cunning a mind as the high priest, when he was inclined to put it to use. Anything, he thought. Anything at all, but get us out of this, or there will be a blood bath and life has suddenly become very important to me. 'Our relationship ended several weeks ago if you remember. Since the night I saw you going to the temple of Ku to sacrifice some poor, innocent little girl. Did you know your sister was a high priestess of the temple?'

'I do—now.'

'Enough,' Kalakui thundered. He could see his advantage rapidly diminishing. 'The *haolewahine* must die. You will also if you interfere.'

'She is your woman, truly?' Tamori asked, moving even closer to Ross. Damn him, Ross thought, he was directly in his line of fire, protecting Kalakui. Was it intentional?

'Yes.' The answer came without hesitation. He could not turn back now.

On the ground Mary Kate moaned as her senses began to return. Looking down at her for an instant, Simon thought he knew the reason for Ross's strange attitude over the past few weeks and why his sister had suddenly returned home when he knew she did not want to. She was not Ross's woman. He had wanted her and she had refused him! Fighting against an attraction for a man different from any she had ever met before, and the teachings of a lifetime. No doubt his father had had a hand in her decision.

'It's up to you what happens next, Tamori. Or to Kalakui, if he's giving the orders and it rather looks as if he is. This is a double-barrelled gun and I have one loaded barrel left. That's for him. Simon, you can have Lani. Don't be squeamish about killing a woman. If she lives and we don't, she'll be the one who tosses your sister into Ku's pit. The rest of you men behind me can choose your own targets. They won't get all of us, that's for sure.'

He had deliberately not given orders to kill Tamori with good reason. He had offered him all the arms and men he could lay his hands on if he chose to go against Kalakui. Now was his opportunity. To prove himself before all the people fearfully watching from the darkness beyond—not seen, or heard, but there all the same—prove he ruled Wameia, that his word alone was law and must be obeyed.

'What will you give up for your woman, my brother?'

Ross's eyes narrowed sharply. The game was on. Lani came up to whisper in Kalakui's ear and was waved angrily back to her place.

'Anything you ask of me.'

'Ross, for God's sake. You don't know what the devil he wants,' Simon hissed worriedly. 'Let's take them and be done with it. We've got to risk it.'

'I'm not going to risk your sister's life, even if you are,' came the terse reply.

'Anything? Give me your ship. You may continue to sail her under my command,' Tamori demanded and

Ross heard an ugly growl run through the men behind him.

'Agreed.' Again, no hesitation with his answer, even though it was his most treasured possession. A ship. What was a ship? The palms of his hands suddenly began to sweat. She was safe! How close he had come to losing her. Foolish, foolish Mary Kate. When would he be able to tell her what was in his heart? Perhaps never!

'You fool!' Lani cried. 'He's lying. I would have known if she had been his.'

'Why?' Ross countered with cool effrontery.

'I am a woman. It would have shown when you made love to me.' Lani stared at him defiantly, open hostility on her face. She knew the depth of his love for the *Moonshadow*, yet he had given it up without a murmur. She began to feel uneasy.

'As it showed you and Kalakui are still lovers?'

She blanched at the words and the hostility became blazing hatred, which momentarily shocked him. Of the two, she was the most dangerous, he now realised. Kalakui's hand began to lift to signal his men. Ross's weapon came up to waist height.

'Try me,' he said and there was murder in the black eyes.

'Will you join with her beneath the *tapa*?' Tamori demanded and Simon gave a strangled oath. 'Was that not your intention when you asked my permission to bring her here?'

'Oh, my God, Ross, what's he trying to do? She'll never agree to that!'

'In her present condition I doubt if she'll know very much about it. Are you going to stop it?' Ross kept his voice low so that it did not carry to those in front of them. 'You know what will happen if I refuse?'

'I can't. I should, but I can't. She'll never forgive you, you know that?'

'I'm used to being on the wrong end of your sister's displeasure,' came Ross's humourless reply. He nodded in Tamori's direction.

'Bring your woman then. One more thing, there will be no more of the "new learning". You will tell her that. She will not interfere in the ways of my people again.'

'Agreed.' She would never forgive him for that either, Ross thought. Lani looked as if she wanted to scratch out his eyes. She would take out her spite on some other poor unfortunate powerless to oppose her, the bitch! Kalakui said nothing, his face expressionless. By remaining silent he also retained the fearful power over the silent people of the village. Astute enough to know he had lost this round, his mind would be searching ahead for another way to destroy those against him. Tamori was marked for certain, but at least he knew it now.

'Mary Kate.' Ross knelt at her side and gently touched the loose hair. She recoiled from his touch as if he had struck her. Her eyes were dull now, blank. She did not recognise him for a full moment, and then she clutched at his shirt.

'Ross. Father!' Her voice rose to a shrill pitch. Tossing his weapon to Simon he drew her to her feet, cradling her against his shoulder. Huge tremors racked her body as her eyes fell on her father's decapitated body and she buried her face against his shoulder, near to fainting again. 'Animals! He went out to them . . .'

Her voice trailed off and she was silent. Terribly silent.

'She's in shock. We've got to get her back to the

house,' Simon urged. 'For God's sake, Ross, her mind could be unhinged by this.'

'Listen, Firehair. You are safe now.' Ross stroked her shoulder and he forced her to walk alongside him towards the middle of the village. Tamori fell into step beside him. Only Lani and Kalakui remained behind. Realising their absence, Tamori turned and the small brown eyes flashed with an authority not often shown in the presence of the high-priest.

'You will come,' was all he said. It was enough. Both began to follow. Last of all came the men from the *Moonflower*, weapons still at the ready. They were not as willing as their Captain to trust the Prince's word. Not when they had to go around the body of Nathaniel Whitney.

'She's sleeping,' Simon said, as he came into the sitting-room and Ross looked up expectantly. 'I've given her the strongest sleeping draught I had. She didn't realise what happened. How could she, poor love. Kept mumbling something about Indian braves.'

'What?' Ross looked at him startled. He rose from the chair where he had been sitting for the past hour, brooding on what had taken place, while upstairs Mary Kate was fussed over by two women and her brother and put quickly to bed. He splashed a large amount of brandy into a glass and pushed it towards the other man. 'You look as if you need it.'

'A whole bottle,' Simon murmured as he tossed it back. 'I'm going to get very drunk.'

'You'll have to put yourself to bed because I'm joining you,' Ross said, replenishing his own glass. He had lost count of how many he had drunk in that hour. 'What's this about Indians?'

'It's something she must have read somewhere, about the Plains Indians at home. When a brave wanted to get married he would stand before the woman of his choice and open the blanket he wore. If she came inside it, they were married.'

'Good God,' Ross ejaculated. 'I didn't think she was that aware of what was happening. Do you think she'll be all right?'

'I don't know. I haven't prayed in years, do you know that, but I found myself praying tonight as I watched her. She's so precious to me, Ross.'

He waited but no answering commitment came.

'Mamalou is staying with her all night,' he added. He sprawled into a chair, stretching his legs out before him and gazing at his dusty boots solemn-faced. 'So now you have a wife and I have a brother-in-law. Somehow I don't feel much like celebrating. No disrespect, Ross. If it had to happen at all, it shouldn't have been this way.'

'Dammit man, do you think I want a wife who can't stand the sight of me?' Ross flung back angrily. 'I was quite happy to stay a bachelor.'

'Were you? Why did you ask Tamori to let her and Father come here then?'

He ignored the pointed remark. Now was no time to analyse his feelings for Mary Kate. They were too confused, too disturbing, too permanent! 'I've had your father's body brought back here. We'll bury him in the morning before she's awake. I thought it better that way. If you agree?'

Simon nodded and continued drinking silently. They spoke little after that, both absorbed in their own intense thoughts. When the bottle was empty, Ross brought another and they consumed it without noticing.

CHAPTER
TEN

EARLY next morning, while Mary Kate lay sleeping under heavy sedation, two sailors from the *Moonflower* dug a grave behind the house and the body of Nathaniel Whitney was lowered into it in a hastily made wooden box. Ross had taken his father's Bible from the study intending Simon should say a few words over his father, but the man shook his head. It was ironical, Ross thought, as he opened the book and began to read from the 23rd Psalm, that he should be the one to do so.

As the coffin was lowered in the hole in the earth, Simon bent and threw a handful of soil after it. Unbeknown to anyone he was praying. For Mamalou, Kiki at his side, Ross and himself and his sister asleep in the house. A prayer that it was not too late for all of them. The drums had been going all night long, ceasing abruptly at daybreak. What had Kalakui in store for them now, he wondered as they made their way back to the house.

Ross's horse was saddled and waiting for him. He wheeled on him with a frown.

'Where are you going?'

'To see Tamori. I said I would last night. We have things to discuss.'

'Back there! Are you crazy? Kalakui's thugs will be waiting for you along the way. I'll come with you.'

'No, you will be needed here if there is going to be trouble, which I doubt. Tamori's stand last night was what a lot of people have been waiting for. I don't think I'm in any danger.' A half-smile touched Ross's face as he swung himself into the saddle. He did not suspect trouble, Simon thought, yet there was his favourite double-barrelled gun beside him and a pistol in his belt. 'Take care of my wife for me.'

'Shall I tell her you said that?'

'Don't be a fool. I'll be back in a couple of hours. Keep everyone working as usual and come down hard on anyone spreading incitement. That Kalakui is capable of just now. I wouldn't put it past him to send in some of his boys to incite our men to rebellion.'

'I'll keep my eyes open, don't worry and if you're not back by noon, I'm coming looking for you.'

'If I'm not back by then, don't bother, you'll be too late,' Ross said as he swung his horse about and Simon swore softly.

Mamalou gently touched his arm. She had an arm around her daughter's shoulders. How he wished he could read her mind. She gave nothing away, Simon thought.

'Come into the house and have some food. There is nothing we can do. He will do what has to be done.'

'Why does he always have to do it alone?' Simon returned in an exasperated tone. 'We are all in danger.'

'He is like his father,' the woman replied softly and the warm brown eyes softened still more at the memories inside her. 'An independent spirit. The *wahine* must learn to recognise this if she wishes to keep him.'

'I'm not sure she does. Besides, she's rather an independent spirit herself, Mamalou. I just wish to God they had met under different circumstances.'

'Are you going to tell her what happened last night?' Kiki asked, slipping her arm about his waist. He smiled down into her apprehensive features, and bent to kiss her on the lips.

'I have the feeling she knows, my love.'

Mary Kate had been awake for some time, but her head ached abominably and she was so drowsy she could hardly move. Her limbs felt like lead. That was the worst part. Her mind was active, but her body did not feel as if it was part of her at all. She forced herself over the pain and horror as she relived those last moments of her father's life and remembered the flames which drove her out to where Kalakui waited, like a hungry vulture. After that everything was very vague. Ross was holding her, speaking to her so gently, his arms so protective around her she had thought it to be a dream. The blanket that had been placed around them had reminded her of something she had read once about the Indians who lived on the Great Plains in America. That was how they chose a bride, by enfolding them inside the blanket they wore.

Slowly she drew herself up in bed, absorbing the shock. By native custom she and Ross were married, she had no doubt of that, but she could not understand why! He had saddled himself with a woman he looked upon only with contempt. It was beyond her comprehension. His wife! No, she was not. Surely he would not, could not consider such a ceremony binding! Yet why not? Was he not a man who took his pleasures where he found them? No, that was not true, either, or he would have taken her beside the pool and not given it a second thought!

She lay back suppressing tears of weariness and confusion. From the doorway, Simon asked quietly,

'Can I come in or would you rather sleep a while longer?'

'No. Please, come and talk to me.' His company would take her mind off those other questions. Questions which only Ross could answer and she knew she would never have the courage to ask him. 'How long have I been asleep?'

'It's eleven o'clock. I gave you rather a heavy sleeping draught. You needed it.' He sat beside her and kissed her cheek. Her pulse beneath his fingers was slow, but her eyes were bright and alert and his fears for her sanity receded into the background.

'I thought you did. My head aches.'

'Fresh air will soon cure that. Could you manage a little food?'

'Not right now.' She did not want to go downstairs and face Ross and he guessed it immediately.

'He is not here, he has gone to see Tamori.'

'Everything is so confused. I remember some things, but the rest . . . Simon, am I married?' Her lips trembled as she asked the question.

Good Lord, he wondered, is she afraid of Ross? He had never considered that. 'Yes. You were married beneath the *tapa*. It was the only way he could save your life. That—and parting with the thing he treasured most.'

She looked at him not understanding for several minutes and then her cheeks blanched.

'The *Moonflower*. No! Why should he part with that for me? I am nothing to him.'

'To save your life. Tamori stepped in to stop Kalakui killing us all. You would have been sacrificed to Ku, had we died.'

'How—how did you know what was happening?' Mary Kate could not grasp what he had said. Given up his beloved ship—for her! Dear God, he really did intend to make her his wife, make her suffer as all the other women he had possessed, as revenge against the mother he had hated!

'Kiki came down to the village with some material to give you for a new dress. She had some very special news to give you too. News she wanted to deliver herself. She saw Kalakui and his men outside the house, and ran back here to get help. We didn't make it in time for Father . . .'

'Oh, Simon,' Mary Kate cried, 'they gave him no chance. He went out there and talked to them. He wanted to die! I don't understand it. In that moment he was willing to give up the lives of us both. He wanted to make them understand why. I don't myself. He was pleased with the school, I know it. He wanted it reopened. Why did he throw away his life?'

Her brother swore beneath his breath and lowered his gaze. When he looked at her again his eyes were filled with pain.

'Perhaps dying for the God he believed in was the only thing left to him. The only thing I had left him.'

'What are you trying to say?' she whispered.

'Kiki's news was that she wished our baby to be baptized. She told Father of this, but he refused. She was not my wife and so the child would be born out of wedlock.'

'That was too cruel of him.'

'Kiki and I are man and wife, Mary Kate. Ross took out to sea in the *Moonflower* the day you opened your school and married us. I told him so the day I tried to persuade him to let you come and live here with us. He had no reason to turn Kiki away ever again. He knew it and had to accept it and baptize our child when it came into the world. It was her idea and I told him so.'

'Did—did you also tell him you would never again be the son he wanted?' She forced the words out, knowing how they would hurt him, knowing also this was a moment of truth between them.

'Yes. He seemed to accept it. He didn't, though, did he? To die for his faith was all I had left him. If you died too there would be another martyr in Heaven. Damn him!'

'Simon, don't! Perhaps in your way you gave him all he has ever wanted. I pray so.'

'Pray,' her brother said harshly. 'Can you still pray after all that has happened to you?'

'I'm not sure. I prayed for God to save Father's life. Not because I loved him, but because it was not right that he be butchered without cause. He did no harm. He blustered and threatened and used people, but in his mind, I believe he considered it God's will. He wanted so much to succeed.'

'He has,' Simon said, grim-faced. 'He can look down on us from his heavenly seat and watch us being murdered because of his stupidity. All this has come about because of the challenge he issued to Kalakui, you know that, don't you?'

'That is only part of it. In time this would have happened anyway, to anyone who came with new ideas. Don't blame him, Simon. Let him sleep in peace.'

'You are too kind. Will you be as kind to Ross, I wonder?'

'You—you have no right to ask that,' Mary Kate returned, her voice hardening. 'Was he not also protecting himself last night?'

'If you think that, then you are a fool! A blind fool.' Simon rose from the bedside. 'I'll have Kiki find you something to wear. Come down and have some food when you are ready and don't speak that way in front of her or Mamalou. He's risked more than his livelihood here saving you. Think about it.'

Mary Kate did not want to think about it. She wanted to keep her thoughts as far as possible away from Ross Pendennis and the fact she was now his property.

At first Ross did not recognise the figure of Mary Kate standing beside the grave of Nathaniel Whitney. He had ridden home, well pleased with what had taken place between himself and Tamori, putting to the back of his mind the final confrontation which must take place to establish his authority in the village and had come out of the trees to see a solitary figure in a green silk *pau* in front of him. He recognised the material instantly, remembering he had brought Kiki a whole bolt of it from one of his trips. And then it suddenly dawned on him, the woman's skin was fair, not brown, and the hair streaming past her shoulders as she turned, was a fiery red! He reined in beside her, watching the bright colour which surged into her face.

For a long moment both were silent, then Ross said pleasantly,

'You don't look as if you have suffered any ill effects from last night. I'm glad.' What an effort it was not to reach out and draw her close to him, tell her what was buried in his heart.

'Are you, Captain?' Her voice was strangely hostile. He had expected tears, shock, even a little gratitude, but her manner was withdrawn. Another wall had gone up between them and he did not understand why. 'You have saddled yourself with an unwanted wife and a lot of trouble you could have avoided, from what Simon tells me.'

'Kalakui is already trying to whip up hysteria among the *kanakas* by demanding your death to appease Ku. They are being threatened with storms, earth-tremors, pestilence until I give you up to him.' He was quite brutal in his reply and saw her wince as it dawned on her how lucky she was still to be alive. It was better she knew how things were going to be. Everyone would have to know and pull their weight in the days ahead until he came back. 'I told them if he didn't behave himself I'd have you speak to Pele and have him devoured by fire.'

'You didn't?' she gasped and he smiled down into her horrified eyes.

'I can do it too, have him devoured by fire, I mean,' he said, in all seriousness. 'But that's my ace in the hole. You know we are married then?'

'We are not!' she stated emphatically. 'Not in my eyes or in the eyes of God. It was a native ceremony and means nothing.'

'We are in Tamori's eyes and those of the villagers and those people are the ones who count at the moment. Don't worry, I'm not going to demand my rights as your husband, I have other, more important things on my mind. Walk back to the house with me, I have news for everyone.'

'Good news?' she ventured to ask, hoping the relief she felt at his words was not too apparent in her expression.

'I think so. At least some of it is.'

He did not enlighten her until they were all seated in the sitting-room, Kiki and Simon close together on the couch, Mamalou and Mary Kate in adjoining chairs. Rose stood with his back to the windows, and lit a cigar before he began.

'The good news is I have my ship back. Tamori was

only putting on a show last night. A damned good one, I admit. He fooled me. This is strictly between us. He wants no one else to know until we have dealt with Kalakui.'

'He's finally decided he will have to stand against him then,' Simon remarked quietly, and felt Kiki's fingers curl around his seeking reassurance. He slipped an arm around her shoulders and drew her closer.

'I'm leaving later this afternoon for the *Moonshadow* and sailing her to Honolulu. I'll be back with as many weapons and as much powder as I can lay my hands on. I'll be taking six, no ten men with me, Simon and you must get organised for when I get back.'

'Organised?' Mary Kate asked in a hollow tone and he looked at her steadily. Since they had entered the room he had deliberately avoided looking at her, not wanting his attention to dwell too long on the way the *tapa* curved over her firm breasts and lithe hips. The way the colour of it made her eyes seem even darker, complementing them with its own richness of colour. She was his, yet they were farther apart than they had ever been. The grin breaking out on Simon's face brought him abruptly back to her question.

'Whatever happens, we shall be ready for it. Find out those we can trust, Simon. I'm having the women belonging to the crew come up here for safety—that's if they want to. Anyone who wants to join with Kalakui can do so, but not one word of the guns is to leak out. We'll arm those we are certain of when I return. The way I see it at the moment, if Kalakui starts anything, he'll be caught between Tamori and his men on one side of the village and us on the other.'

'If they get to the house, we are vulnerable from three sides,' Simon reminded him and Ross nodded grimly.

'I've thought of that. We'll discuss it later. I have a few surprises up my sleeve, not even you know about. Mamalou, you've been through this kind of thing before. You and Kiki take care of the house and things we may need.'

'What—what can I do?' Mary Kate asked hesitantly. She felt she had been deliberately left out.

'This is not your fight. Why should you do anything? I'll try and arrange a passage back home for you when I'm in Honolulu. You'll be safe here until then. This thing isn't going to blow up overnight. Kalakui needs time to incite enough fear and hatred into the villagers first.'

'What makes you think it will blow up anyway?' Simon asked, while Mary Kate sat thunderstruck. He was sending her away! He had no right. She belonged here as much as he did! It was her home! 'You seem very sure.'

Ross drew deeply on his cigar, aware too of the dazed expression on her face. She looked for all the world as if she cared about leaving.

'Tamori received word early this morning from the Big Island that Kamehameha is very ill. Liholiho is massing an army to support him as the new king. If the old man does die, the old ways will die with him. Unfortunately, the messenger never reached his boat to return with an acclamation of loyalty. His body was found behind the Hut of Sacred Secrets. Kalakui's hut! We can safely assume we are not the only ones in possession of the news. I'm to be the bearer of the tidings.'

'Be careful,' Mamalou warned. 'At such times it is difficult to know friends from enemies.'

'You should know better than to worry about me.

Besides only the good die young, isn't that right, Mary Kate?' He fixed her with a mocking smile. 'It's going to be a long time before anyone up there wants to call me from this earth.'

Mary Kate could not stand the smile which crossed his features. She fought against the love within her which she had tried so hard to ignore—to deny—which rose up inside her once again until she had to bite her lip to stop herself begging him to take care. Beneath the startled gaze of four pairs of eyes, she ran out of the room.

'Why don't you tell Mary Kate you love her,' Simon murmured and watched the smile immediately vanish from Ross's face.

'I don't know how.'

Three long days without him! Endless hours of pretending before the others she did not miss him! At the end of them, Mary Kate felt drained of energy and vitality. The slightest sound from outside sent her rushing to the window to see if he was returning. Mamalou and Kiki, if they noticed her growing agitation, showed no signs. They gave her jobs to do about the house to keep her busy from early in the morning until late at night. She discovered after a while, they had been busily sorting through linen and sheets suitable for the making of bandages. Stockpiling food and other necessities inside the house and bringing many of the animals within the paling. As if they were to undergo a siege, she thought apprehensively. How calm they were, always smiling, always with a cheerful word for her, making her ashamed of her own thoughtless attitude. She voiced her intention of working with them and her offer was not refused. The next day she found herself tearing up sheets and that was how Ross found her when he came back.

'Kamehameha is dead,' he told them when they were all together. Mary Kate saw lines of tiredness beneath his eyes and there was a growth of beard on his chin as if he had not been concerned with the little, unimportant things during his absence. 'The islands are in an uproar. Liholiho has a strong following, but not so strong he can spare men to come back with me. At least not yet. The *Amber Queen* was in harbour, still with Captain Johnston in command, thank heavens. He's bringing additional powder and he's offered to fight alongside us if it becomes necessary.'

'Out of our sixty men, we can count on forty. I've sent the rest packing, families and all,' Simon informed him. 'I didn't think this was a time for weakness,' he added as Ross frowned. 'But we've gained four families from the village which gives us back eleven men. I've just seen what you brought back. We have a small arsenal here now. Kalakui can't match anything like this.'

'War canoes followed me back here,' Ross said, 'and they are not on Tamori's side. Liholiho made no bones about the fact the temples will come down and the high priests will be out of work, but the young fool spoke up too early and gave warning to all those who oppose him. They've been planning rebellion for weeks, even before the old King became ill. He's going to have a bloody fight on his hands. Who knows how long it will last? The women will leave first thing tomorrow and there will be no exceptions,' he added sternly as Mamalou's face became decidedly obstinate. 'You have to look after Kiki and the baby for Simon and see Mary Kate gets safely aboard her ship. Duncan will give you all the details,' he added, looking across to where she sat, a torn sheet across her lap. His mind was closed against her impending departure and the loss he must endure. It had been of his own making and he would suffer for it to the end of his days. 'Before you leave I'll give you a letter of credit to a bank in Boston. You'll have enough to settle down and go back to teaching. That's what you want isn't it?'

No, it isn't, she wanted to scream at him, but she only nodded, too miserable to do otherwise with so many eyes on her. There was nothing for her in Boston, or anywhere else in the world without him. Her place was here. She had accepted that a few hours after he left, had been summoning courage to approach him when he had shattered her with his announcement. He did not want her. Why should he? He did not have Lani any longer, but she was a mere shadow in comparison. Certainly no alternative to the passionate princess who had held him for two years.

Kiki swore she would not leave. Ross ignored her and proceeded to continue discussing the arrangements with Mamalou. The girl cried, stormed, threatened, but to no avail. Neither he nor Simon relented, even though she knew it broke her brother's heart to be away from his wife for even a few short hours. Eventually Mamalou took her upstairs to gather together some clothes and Kiki went with her, still tearful, but exhausted and in silent acceptance of the fact she must leave.

'You should get an early night too,' Ross said to Mary Kate and the words she wanted to say failed to materialise as she stared into his black eyes and found nothing there to give her encouragement. Without a word she rose and followed them.

In the cold, grey light of dawn as the first streaks of light seared the sky, the crowd of people gathering before the house were silent, solemn-faced. The men had their spears and knives, the women a few belongings. Many clutched infants in their arms. Ross stepped out on to the verandah and faced then, a sinking feeling in his heart. He had been too quick to count on their loyalty. They were an ignorant, fear-ridden people and faced with the prospect of Kalakui's wrath, the damnation of their gods and a horrible death if they were caught in open rebellion, they had chosen to return to the village. He counted them without a word. Less than twenty men left in addition to the few of his crew who had arrived last night. Maybe he would ask Mary Kate to say a prayer for him before she left.

'The ungrateful swines,' Simon muttered, watching them slowly turn away and stream towards the gates. 'What were they waiting for anyway?'

'For me to see them. They knew I would understand,' Ross answered quietly. He absorbed the shock of his position and put it to the back of his mind. He was not beaten yet!

'Understand? Why didn't you try to stop them? We need them.'

'We need men who will stay until the end. We'd have to watch each and every one of them if I tried to keep them here by force. Don't tell the women. Quiet, here they come.'

'I'm coming back as soon as they are on board,' Simon said tersely. 'Don't argue.'

'I had no intention of doing so, I'm not that much of a fool. Thanks.'

'Why are you sending Mary Kate away?'

'I have to. For God's sake, Simon, I'm not exactly a paragon of virtue, am I? She hates everything I've ever done. Everything I do,' he corrected, his eyes looking past his companion to the slender girl who had just emerged from the house. 'She has no life here with me.

She was meant for better things.'

'Don't you think she should be the judge of that? Ask her. Or shall I?'

'If you open your mouth and say one word to her, don't ever come back,' Ross snapped. 'Now get them out of here. I've work to do.'

Not a word of gentleness as they parted. He neither touched her, nor showed any sign of regret at her leaving. For Kiki and Mamalou there were hugs and kisses, given with warmth and tenderness on his face. For her, an assurance only, that she would be well taken care of in Honolulu and on board ship. She took the envelope he handed her, wanting to tear it into shreds before his eyes, but knowing it would be a meaningless gesture and achieve nothing.

'Goodbye, Captain Pendennis.' How formal she was. Playing his game out to the last. 'I will pray for you.'

'I was hoping you might,' Ross said, with a crooked smile and went back into the house, leaving Simon to help her on to her horse.

They caught up with the tail-end stragglers from the plantation less than ten minutes later and it suddenly dawned on all three women how few men were left behind to defend the house.

'Don't look at me like that,' Simon said with a scowl as they all turned on him. 'It was his choice. He didn't even try to talk to them.'

'You can,' Mary Kate pleaded. 'Make them go back. He needs them.'

'He needs us all.' Mamalou urged her horse on until she was abreast with several of the men. They heard her voice raised in anger as she berated them for their desertion of the man who had given them homes, food, a living far above anything they had ever known before.

Had been a friend more than an employer, caring for their families when they were sick, allowing them to retain their jobs if they themselves were ill or injured. Allowing them, and never interfering, to pray to the savage gods they knew he did not acknowledge.

They rode on to join her and when she looked at them, her face was quivering with rage.

'They go because of you.' She looked directly at Mary Kate. Never before had she shown she was capable of such intense emotion. Her huge frame actually shook in the saddle. 'The "chosen one of Pele" has deserted her man. Why should these *kanakas* risk their lives for him, when she will not?'

'Oh, no!' Kiki cried. 'It is not her fault. She is not one of us.'

'But I am.' Mary Kate drew herself upright, her blue eyes bright with sapphire fire. 'They are right. I should not have allowed him to send me away. Tell them I am going back, Mamalou. Tell them it is Pele's wish they return with me. Tell them . . .' she hesitated, remembering Ross's words of a few nights ago. 'If they disobey me, if they run back to Kalakui like frightened children, I will have Pele destroy not only him, but them too with her fire and all their wives and children. She will open the Big Mountain once again and their bodies will be washed away in the red-hot river which comes down from it. Tell them this and make them believe it.'

'Make them believe it,' Simon ejaculated. 'Holy Moses, Mary Kate, you've got me believing it. If only you could see the way you look! I wish Ross could.'

'He will soon enough. I love him, Simon. I'll stay with him even though he doesn't want me.'

'Ask him if he wants you. The answer might not be the one you are expecting.'

Sudden hope dawned on her features, but there was apprehension too, that his words did not mean her hopes and dreams would become reality. That Ross might actually care for her!

'They will go back with you and stay as long as you stay,' Mamalou said, the sternness disappearing from her face. 'We will all go back. We are a family.'

'Wait! I think it might be wise to find out what's happening in the village.' Simon singled out a young *kanaka* and spoke to him for a few minutes. The man made off into the trees and he came back to them. 'I've sent him to do a little spying. He'll try and get back to us by nightfall.'

Mary Kate felt her mouth begin to grow dry as they turned about and began to return to the house. Now she had made the mammoth decision she was beginning to be fearful of how she would be received. What if he tried to send her away again, even when she said she loved him? No, he could not do that! But he could, and he might!

'Let me go on ahead,' she begged as they reached the outside of the paling, the tall, sturdy bamboo fencing which she knew Ross was depending on to prevent a headlong attack on the house itself. If he scorned her, mocked her admission of love, she wanted no one else there to hear it. She could spare herself that final humiliation at least.

'Go ahead,' Simon urged, with an encouraging smile. Kiki reached out and kissed her on her cheeks, her eyes shining. Mamalou said nothing, but something near to satisfaction registered in her expression as she watched the girl proceed on into the compound.

Mary Kate, rehearsing what she would say, had the words dashed from her mind as the door was flung open and Ross strode out to face her, hands on his hips. His face was as dark as thunder and her courage began to crumble.

'What the devil are you doing here?' he demanded ungraciously and she was shocked at the harshness of his voice. Again that faint hope rose inside her to instil fresh confidence. Why did he stand there glaring at her so furiously if he was not pleased to see her and at the same time, afraid for her safety?

'You are going to need all the help you can get,' she said bravely. 'Even mine.'

'No! Not yours,' he flung back, eyes flashing.

'What about theirs then?' She turned and looked back towards the gates where the others waited and then at Ross again, watching the incredulity which spread across his face slowly replaced by a look of immense relief. He was not alone, left with a mere handful of men to defend all that was precious to him. Mamalou, Kiki, Simon! All his men that had left were coming back towards the house. It was no dream. They were as real as—as the bright-eyed figure astride the horse facing him, who he had thought never to see again.

'You,' he said. 'Why are you here?'

'My place is beside my husband,' Mary Kate declared with a calmness that surprised even her. The dark eyes narrowed in disbelief.

'We are not man and wife in the eyes of God.'

Mary Kate took a deep breath, knowing she must say what was in her heart quickly before she had a large audience.

'I once said to you, if you love this place you will fight for it. You are going to do just that. I happen to love you, Ross, and I consider that worth fighting for too.' There, now he knew. Why didn't he say something? Why was he looking at her so strangely? 'You can't send me away again. If—if you do, I'll come back again and again until . . . until . . .'

'Is it worth dying for?' Ross interrupted white-faced. Only once before had he come so close to losing his self-control and that had been that day at the pool when he had held her in his arms and felt her close to surrender and known if he took advantage of her, it would be the most dishonourable thing he had ever done in his life. So he had sent her away from him and shut out of his mind, his life, the knowledge that he was capable of love. Something he had never thought possible. Not the kind of love that meant commitment forever, settling down with one woman, remaining faithful because he was content with the woman he had. He had found it and been unable to admit it and take that final, binding step. It no longer frightened him. Nor was it a challenge, which was why he did most things in his life.

'With you? Yes.' She did not hesitate with her answer. 'I know I am not Lani, but I can learn. I am sure you would be a very good teacher.' The boldness of her words brought a flush of colour to her otherwise pale cheeks. 'You have two fights on your hands now.'

'First I'll deal with Kalakui and then you shall have my undivided attention,' Ross assured her, adding grimly. 'Providing we are still alive.'

He stretched out his arms and she slid into them and then, in a final, reckless gesture leant up on tiptoe and kissed him.

'Just to make sure you don't forget,' she said, before running into the house her cheeks now redder than an island sunset.

'I would consider that a definite invitation,' Simon remarked as he drew rein beside his friend.

Ross's eyes began to gleam as he stared up at the three faces smiling at him. Each and every one registering outright approval.

'Get the men back to work. I'll be down in a while,' he grinned and started after Mary Kate.

'Ross, what are you doing? Let me go this instant!' He grabbed her hand as she stood trembling in the kitchen, unable to believe she was still there after speaking to him so boldly, and started towards the stairs, pulling her after him. What was he going to do? Her heart almost failed her as she looked into the wicked, gleaming eyes and knew exactly what he intended for her. 'Simon, stop him, he's gone mad.' Desperately she appealed to Simon who lounged in the doorway with Kiki and Mamalou beside him. No one seemed in the least concerned with her predicament. It was not proper. Not yet!

Her brother's hearty laughter followed her up the stairs and into the corridor which led to the study. Hampered by her long skirts, Mary Kate tripped and almost fell. Ross scooped her up into his arms and continued on without pausing in his long strides.

'Ross, no!' She breathed, but already her resolve was weakening. 'We must wait.'

'You came back to be my wife,' he said quietly, almost gently. 'Whatever happens, no one will be able to take this moment away from us. I may have but a little time to show you how much I love you.'

With a soft cry Mary Kate clung to him, frightened by the implication behind those last words, but as he bent and kissed her, the fear vanished instantly. Her fingers entwined in his thick blond hair as her lips parted beneath his, answering his kiss for kiss. Shouldering open the door of the room beyond, Ross carried her inside, to lay her on the huge canopied bed where he had never lain with another woman. To show her, in the long hours of passion and revelation which followed, the depth of his love and to acknowledge in return, the great prize which was his.

'I must go and do some work.' Mary Kate stirred sleepily as he moved away from her. The room was filled with sunlight and she realised it was quite late. Time had been unimportant for them. 'Stay here for a while.'

'No. I'm coming to help,' she insisted and he looked down at her amusedly.

'Are you going to be a troublesome wife?'

'No. Faithful and obedient.' He loved her!

She did not meet his gaze and he knew instantly what was on her mind. Smoothing the tangled curls away from her face he kissed her on the mouth, allowing his lips to travel down to the smooth line of her throat before quickly drawing back. It would be so easy to linger beside her and abandon his work to others while he enjoyed the delights of this new-found love, but he must not.

'When Captain Johnston gets here with the *Amber Queen* and all this is over, we'll be married the way you want. All the right words. I've lived here for fifteen years and I've lived by island rules, but if it makes you happy, you'll have the proper ceremony and afterwards the biggest *luau* Oahu has ever seen. If you like I'll even invite the new King and all his court.'

'Just a ring that means I am your wife forever,' Mary Kate whispered softly. He understood!

Rising, he crossed to the bureau against one wall, pulled out one of the drawers and took something out. A smile on his lips, he took her hand and slipped on to her wedding finger a thick gold band.

'I found this in the ashes of the hut. I thought you would want it. I'll buy you one as soon as possible, but perhaps you would like to wear this until then?'

'Oh, bless you! It was my mother's. Ross, why were you sending me away?'

'Why? Because you hated the kind of life I've led here, my association with Lani. Despised me for that day beside Pele's pool when I discovered how much has been missing from my life. I know now I would have come after you wherever you went. You have given yourself a life-long sentence, my darling. I'll never let you go now.'

After he had left her Mary Kate quickly dressed and ran a brush over her dishevelled hair. Her eyes fell on the wedding ring she wore and she laid her lips against it with a sigh. No experience in the world, she thought as she went downstairs, could be as beautiful or as satisfying as for a woman to lie in the arms of the man she loved and have her love returned. It was a gift from God and she had accepted it unconditionally.

The sound of an explosion way off in the distance halted her on the stairs. Her hand flew to her mouth in silent terror. Were they under attack? No, it was nearer the village than the house. Another? It sounded like cannon-fire, but that could not be, unless . . . Her heart lurched unsteadily. Had the war canoes from the Big Island launched an attack on the *Moonshadow*, their last avenue of escape if all did not go well here?

'Simon, what is happening?' She ran after her brother on to the verandah. Mamalou and Kiki were arm in arm out there already and Ross came running towards them from one of the smoke-houses.

'I'm not sure. It might be the *Amber Queen* warning us she has dropped anchor. That means more men and arms.'

'No,' Ross said, with a shake of his head. 'I think not. Look.'

Over the tall trees which soared high into the sky beyond the paling billowed dense black smoke and then fierce red flames. Mary Kate went to him and slipped her hand into his, trying to hide her fear.

'Isn't that from the village?' she ventured to ask. What dreadful thing had taken place?

'I took the precaution of leaving something more with Tamori than powder and guns. He still does not have enough men to rout Kalakui and the longer the fight, the more chance others will go over to the other side and desert him. I'm praying he's used what I gave him and in doing so, has established himself as ruler here. No longer weak, but strong beyond dispute, able to deal ruthlessly with those who have gone against him. It may save a fight here if he does.'

'Just what was that?' Simon asked, moving to the edge of the verandah steps. 'To make that amount of smoke and flame . . .'

'A present from my old friend Wong.'

'The Chinese merchant? What was in that box he gave you the day after you saved his life?'

'Age-old secrets he would have passed on to his son, had he had one. Medicinal some of them, how to cure everything from a cold to gout. And something very special. How to make "Greek Fire".'

'Good lord,' Simon said in a stunned voice. 'Is that what you were mixing up just now in the smoke-house? In all those little bottles? That could do—that!' He turned back towards the column of smoke, shaking his head.

'It's highly volatile stuff, that's why I had it hidden in a place no one would find it. You might recall I keep putting off rebuilding the smoke-house. If I lit a fire in there, I'd blow us all to kingdom come.' Ross chuckled. Mary Kate marvelled at his ingenuity and daring and his calmness. He had arranged all that without saying a word to any of them. He felt her eyes on him and smiled. 'It might not have worked. For all I know Tamori has blown himself sky-high, not his enemies.'

'I don't think so,' Simon pointed towards the gate where Hopi was waving wildly. 'Someone's coming. You four men, go and see who it is. Quickly. You women, get inside, just in case.'

Ross nodded agreement and as much as she wanted to stay, Mary Kate withdrew to the safety of the house, but no further than the doorway, from where she could see both men clearly as they armed themselves and approached the gates. *Kanakas* converged towards the paling on all sides, armed with guns, hatchets, spears. If there was to be a fight, it would be long and bloody and there was no one to say who the winner would be. There would be many dead and injured on both sides. In war there was no winner, she decided.

Another explosion from beyond the trees. Not from the village this time, but from the direction of the sea. She heard her brother give an enthusiastic holler and shout,

'The *Amber Queen!*'

Extra help had arrived. If only it was not too late. If Kalakui and his men were outside threatening them, the crew from the ship might find they had arrived too late, for it would take them at least three hours to make the overland trek to the house. So much could happen in that time! Ross might be injured—or killed! No, she must not think of that.

The gates were opened, people were streaming in.

She heard Mamalou gasp behind her and turned to see tears running down her brown face. Kiki's cheeks too were wet. There was shouting and slapping of backs as *kanakas* from the outside fell on to those inside and instead of attacking them—embraced them. She passed a trembling hand over her eyes. Was she imagining all this? Was there to be no fight after all?

'Ross! Ross!' Picking up her skirts she ran after him, unable to bear the uncertainty a moment longer. She was caught up in his arms and whirled high into the air and then gathered against his chest and kissed, slowly and lingeringly.

'Tamori did it! He fired the powder trail I laid at exactly the right time and blew Kalakui and most of his men to eternity. Now everyone is really convinced you and Pele are on talking terms.'

'I don't understand.'

'Do you remember I threatened Kalakui with Pele's anger, that you'd ask her to consume him with fire? Well, when the powder reached the naphtha bottles, that's exactly what happened.'

'How horrible!'

'Was his death any worse than the one he planned for you? Don't waste sympathy on him. It's over. His power is broken. By tomorrow Tamori will have established himself in his place. The war canoes that followed me turned back when they heard of the guns and powder he had. Captain Johnston will have taken care of them.'

'And Lani?'

'She died too. She was at his side. It was her choice.' His voice was emotionless. It was as if he had never known her. He knew she would not have shed a tear at his demise. 'I'll take half the men and go to the village to help Tamori clear up. This job has to be done properly if we are to avoid further trouble. You may get your school yet. I'll need Simon too. Will you greet Captain Johnston and entertain him until we get back? We need him remember. I still have to make an honest woman of you. After that you can spend the rest of your life trying to reform me. I'm not guaranteeing any success mind, but it might be fun,' he teased gently.

'I love you as you are. I don't want you ever to change.' Mary Kate blushed as he looked down into her shining blue eyes. She would always blush, she thought, when he looked at her with such intense longing in his eyes and every nerve in her body began to tingle in anticipation of the love they would once again share. Day after day. Night after night, until the end of time.

'Why, Mary Kate, I do believe there is a chance for you yet,' Ross chuckled as he bent his head to take possession of the soft mouth upturned and waiting for his own.